DELILAH AND THE DEEP BLUE SEA

Michaela Francis

DELILAH AND THE DEEP BLUE SEA

Prologue

Robin Hood's Bay, England, January 2009: -

The north easterly wind blew bitterly across the dark headland, whipping the crests of the blackened waves to foam as they marched in ranks into the Bay to expand their energy on the protective walls and slipway of the tiny old smuggler's village and to splash the steps of the Bay Hotel in salt water spray. The high spring tide had brought the cold North Sea to the very feet of the cluster of brick cottages that clung precipitously to the cleft in the slate clay cliffs. Many houses of the old village had long since disappeared; swallowed by the relentless erosion of the cliffs. Those that remained, huddled behind the new sea defences that afforded them some longer lease of life but it was a precarious armed truce on this exposed stretch of the North Yorkshire coast. It seemed a fragile truce indeed on this wild dark night, for the village felt tiny and vulnerable, its narrow cobbled streets lit insufficiently by occasional street lamps that shook in the high wind and served only to illuminate small patches of wet flagstones and the sheets of sleet driving in from the sea.

In a small cottage, a little way up the steep cobbled street that wound its way down from the cliff top to the waves crashing on the boat ramp, a light yet burned in a small window. In the tiny living room of the cottage, Dr Delilah Delmonte sat at a desk with the letter spread out before her. Ngam was reclining on the couch before the coal fire pretending to read a book yet eyeing Delilah worriedly. Rufus, the big red setter was curled up on the hearth rug before the fire asleep, his legs twitching occasionally as he relived the day's adventures along the beach of the bay in his dreams. It was snug and cosy in the little living room. The cadence of the waves on the

5

foreshore were but a distant rumble and the tiny cottage a haven of warm security stirred only by the muted roar of the gale in the rafters and the streaks of sleet on the windows.

Delilah and Ngam loved these interludes together when they could escape from the house in Cambridge to spend a few days alone, far from the obligations of work and family. The little rented cottage in Robin Hood's Bay on the North Yorkshire coast was a favourite of theirs, especially in the winter months when the little village was mercifully free of tourists. They'd spend their days walking Rufus along the beach to Boggle Hole and exploring the rock pools with the wind in their hair and the hiss of the surf on the rocks. In the evenings they'd nurse a glass of ale in front of the big fire in the snug bar of the Bay Hotel or simply enjoy each other's company in the cottage and count themselves blessed. They were interludes of togetherness and times to glory in nothing else other than the love that had bonded these two remarkable women together for so many years.

It was inevitable of course that they would spend such interludes by the sea for the sea held a very special place in both their hearts and especially that of Delilah's. Delilah's life work had its origins in the mysteries of the sea, a dedication that bordered on an obsession that had haunted her for over thirty five years. The sea called to her with a special call; a siren's call.

Ngam laid her book aside with a sigh. "Well I guess we're not going to get to bed any time soon." she observed ruefully. "Not until you get whatever it is off your chest anyway."

Delilah nodded regretfully. "I'm sorry honey. It's just this damned letter." The letter had arrived at the cottage this morning, forwarded from the institution that sponsored Delilah's research. In the normal course of events, routine mail could wait until they returned home to Cambridge but this letter came direct from the institution and was possessed of authority and priority. It was a letter that could not be ignored.

"What's in that letter anyway?" asked Ngam with a frown. "You've been moping over the blasted thing all day."

"It's from some guy in California I've never heard of."

"So? Nothing earth shaking there. What's he want?"

Delilah turned to look at Ngam. "It's a contact sweetheart! One of the best reports we've had in years!"

Ngam's big brown eyes opened wide at the news. "Oh my! Can you share it?"

Delilah nodded and passed the letter over. Communications concerning this subject were usually deep secrets to be seen only by people with the proper clearance from the institution but Delilah shared everything with Ngam. Carefully Ngam began to read.

**

"Dear Doctor Delmonte,

Please forgive me for writing to you without the formality of having been previously introduced. In fact I have your name from Doctor William Bloomingdale, lecturer in marine biology at the University of California, Santa Barbara. I have recounted the events which I will shortly describe to you to Doctor Bloomingdale and he urged me to forward the story to yourself. He tells me that he has collaborated with you a number of times over the past few years and that you have a particular interest in certain aspects of marine ecology and he feels that the story I have to recount falls within your specific sphere of expertise.

Allow me to introduce myself. My name is Stuart Bell and I am a marketing consultant with a leading Los Angeles firm. I am no expert on marine biology and ecology other than through amateur interest. My interest in the subject is a result of my passion for salt water fly fishing; a pastime I have pursued for many years. It is this pastime that led me directly to the encounter which has so haunted me this past couple of years.

Before I recount my tale I will ask you, at least, to hear my story without any prejudgement and in the knowledge that I am attempting to relate the details of the incident as faithfully and as accurately as I can. I am not a fanciful person Dr Delmonte. I pride myself on my sobriety and rationality. I don't believe in UFOs, crop circles, alien conspiracy theories or any other of the nonsense for which the State of California seems famous. I have always considered myself to be the sort of person that can look at anything and subject it to a rational analysis and formulate conclusions based upon level headed judgement. That is until the events of five years ago.

Five years ago, I joined the Clipperton Exploratory Expedition sailing on the "Royal Star" out of Cabo san Lucas in Baja California, Mexico. The Royal Star is a hundred foot chartered fishing vessel, specially configured to the requirements of long distance expeditions of this nature. I joined around twenty other fly anglers on what was hoped to be a serious expedition to the remote Pacific atoll of Clipperton Island lying nearly 600 miles south east of the Revillagigedo archipelago and perhaps some eight to nine hundred miles west of Mexico. The waters around this isolated and uninhabited island are pristine and virtually untouched by either commercial or sport fishermen. Everything we knew about it suggested that the fishing would be terrific and probably yield some world records for the anglers on the expedition.

The voyage to Clipperton took over three days although we did pause for a while to sample the tuna fishing around Islas Revillagigedo before pressing on southward for Clipperton. The fishing off the Revillagigedo archipelago was a little disappointing although we didn't stay long enough to explore it fully to be fair. Most of our hopes were centred on the seas around Clipperton.

Clipperton Island is just about the most isolated and barren piece of real estate you could wish to come across. It's a coral ring atoll and the whole land surface of it amounts to no more than about three and a half square miles. The ring itself is nowhere more than around 400 yards wide, completely encircling a stagnant freshwater lagoon. Most of it is just pretty barren coral sand a few feet above sea level but there is one outcropping of volcanic rock down in the south east of it called "Clipperton Rock" which rises to around 95 feet.

The central lagoon is quite deep in places falling away to over 140 feet but it is stagnant and virtually lifeless. Although the water is fresh water it has usually been regarded as non-potable. This view of it was challenged however following the shipwreck of the tuna clipper MV Monarch in 1962 whose crew survived on the water in the lagoon for some 23 days before being rescued. Although ordinarily we might consider the water as unfit to drink it does seem that it can be drunk if necessary. Dr Bloomingdale seems to regard this latter point as significant.

The vegetation on the island is generally sparse and scrubby; just a sparse cover of spiny grass and low scrubby plants. There are a few stands of coconut palms that survive from the plantations that were planted by guano miners at the end of the 19th century but I think there are supposed to be less than 700 palms on the whole island and most of the place is a pretty arid, desert sort of landscape.

This is not to say that it is devoid of life. Far from it. One thing that you notice straight away are the crabs. There are thousands upon thousands of these bright orange crabs crawling over the landscape. They're reputed to be poisonous but the same guano miners that introduced the palms also introduced pigs to the island and these seemed to eat the crabs with no problems at all. In fact they tell me that the pigs predation of the crabs altered the entire ecology of the island in the early years of the 20th century. The crabs, you see, eat pretty much anything and it's their rapaciousness that reduces the vegetation on the island. With the introduction of pigs the numbers of crabs fell dramatically and for a short time at least the islands became much more lush with vegetation. It was only when these pigs were finally eradicated from the island in 1958 that the numbers of crabs were able to proliferate to their former abundance and reduce the island once more to its semi barren state.

The other notable life on the island are the birds. There are huge colonies of nesting sea birds on Clipperton including White Terns, Sooty Terns, Brown Boobies, Black Noddies, Greater Frigatebirds and Brown Noddies. Perhaps the most numerous are the colonies of Masked Boobies. Some 110,000 of them rear their young on the island all year round. The birds have absolutely no fear of man and you can walk straight through the middle of their vast colonies, deafened by their raucous calls. It is this vast conglomeration of sea birds of course that leaves so much guano on the island as to have historically made the mining of it an attractive commercial enterprise.

The history of the island is quite interesting. It was originally discovered in 1711 by two French explorers, Martin de Chassiron and Michel du Bocage. These two explorers were the commanders of the ships La Princesse and La Decouverte which explored the area in the early 18th century. They named the island Ile de la Passion (Passion Island) and claimed it for France. It was uninhabited then and remained so until a brief period of habitation by a scientific expedition under

Bocage in 1725. The island's English name comes from the English pirate and privateer John Clipperton who reputedly used the island as a base for his attacks on Spanish shipping in the Eastern Pacific in the early 18th century although the documentary evidence for this is slim.

Otherwise there is nothing to suggest that any people disturbed the colonies of nesting birds until the island's ownership came under dispute in the 19th century. In that century the harvesting of guano as fertiliser became big business and the otherwise uninteresting island suddenly became valuable real estate by virtue of the copious bird droppings on the island. Our fellow countrymen were at the forefront of this new commercial interest with the American Guano Mining Company claiming the rights to the island under the Guano Islands Act passed by Congress in 1856. This was a handy little piece of imperialistic legislation by our government that gave US citizens the right to take possession of any uninhabited island containing guano deposits. This law states;

> *"Whenever any citizen of the United States discovers a deposit of guano on any island, rock, or key, not within the lawful jurisdiction of any other Government, and not occupied by the citizens of any other Government, and takes peaceable possession thereof, and occupies the same, such island, rock, or key may, at the discretion of the President, be considered as appertaining to the United States."*

It was of course pretty much a bare faced land grab and, had any other nation done the same, our government would have probably howled blue murder. In fact, at around this time, Mexico joined the fray and claimed the island for no other reason than it happened to be the closest nation to it. France re-iterated its own claim under Napoleon III and, from being pretty much a worthless lump of coral in the middle of nowhere, the island suddenly became desirable property. This squabble continued for the rest of the 19th century with first American and then Mexican miners occupying the island with some French intervention as well and in fact the full question of sovereignty was not finally settled until 1931 in favour of the French claim. It remains a sovereign French territory.

By this time the island had already undergone colonisation. In 1906 the British Island Pacific Island Company had obtained the guano mining rights from Mexico and built, in conjunction with the Mexicans, a settlement for the miners and their families. By 1914 over 100 people were settled on the island. This colonisation ended in disaster and tragedy. By 1917 virtually all the men on the island were dead of scurvy or attempts to escape from a tropical "paradise" that had in fact turned out to be a barren trap. The last man alive, the lighthouse keeper Victoriano Alvarez, seems to have been quite mad for he declared himself "king" and lorded it over the remaining 15 women and children using them for his sexual pleasure in an orgy of rape and depravity until one woman, Tirza Rendon, having an aversion to his sexual attentions, killed him. The surviving four women and seven children were finally evacuated by the American gunship USS Yorktown in July 1917.

Thereafter, apart from brief occupations in the 1930s and American military occupation in 1944-5 during World War Two the island has remained uninhabited once more. I have gone into the history of the island at some length because I think it is important to emphasise that this island has always been unoccupied. There is no evidence ever of any traditional indigenous Pacific Island population and the occupations of the island by foreigners to the region has been brief and short lived. The islands therefore have always been considered uninhabited. My story however might raise questions about the exact definition of "uninhabited" in this instance.

If the vegetation on the island is sparse and its animal life restricted to crabs, birds and a few lizards and rats there is one place there where life is abundant indeed. The seas around Clipperton and its coral reefs are teeming with life. Indeed it is the prolific abundance of the fish in the sea about the island that provides the nourishment for those hundreds of thousands of nesting birds. It was this virtually untapped abundance that our expedition aboard the Royal Star was attracted by.

Upon arriving at the island, we anchored in the lee of the island to the east. There is of course no natural harbour on Clipperton. It was in excited anticipation that we began to cast our flies into the sea around the vessel. To begin with we fished directly from the open decks of the Royal Star. We were not limited to this however for we had two large inflatable powered dinghies aboard, which could be launched to fish away from the mother ship. These were useful too whenever a large fish was hooked from aboard the mother vessel for it was impracticable for the Royal Star to chase any long running fish and it was necessary for the angler to debark into one of the dinghies to pursue the quarry.

I have to say right at the start that the fishing was everything we had expected of the place. It had been a hope that we might claim new world records for fly tackle around Clipperton. It was beyond even our wildest hopes though that we would claim our first world record within a couple of hours of commencing fishing. To begin with in the early hours of the morning we hooked into numerous Yellow Finned Tuna; bruising battlers on our fly tackle averaging over thirty pounds apiece. As the sun rose higher however the tuna moved more offshore and were replaced by shoals of another pelagic species.

Rainbow Runner are beautiful hard fighting game fish. When I've caught them before they've averaged about six pounds. The ones off Clipperton were simply unreal. At that time the world record Rainbow Runner on a fly rod had weighed 10lbs 12ozs. The first one aboard at Clipperton weighed over 16 pounds! It was an awesome fish destroying the old record. The new record lasted less than thirty minutes before an even bigger one came inboard. It was the fly angling stuff of dreams.

We fished the water around the island for several days and it was pure magic. The tuna were extraordinary with big Yellowfins and smaller Black Finned Tuna. The big Yellow Finned in particular gave us some memorable battles. I chased one in the dinghy for an hour and half before finally losing it. I even hooked a big Wahoo that led me another song and dance. Each night we would collapse into our bunks aboard the Royal Star exhausted from the madcap action; our arms aching from playing fish.

If it had only been the fishing then the trip would have been memorable in itself. It was an incident on our last day at Clipperton however that truly etched the whole expedition into my memory. It is an incident I must, in fairness, tell you that nobody else aboard, bar perhaps one, believed and, had someone else reported it, I doubt whether I would have believed it myself.

One of the things we did during our visit to the island was to land people on the island and thus allow them to fish from the beach within the confines of the outlying reef. This gave the opportunity to fish for other species of fish more associated with the reef and less of the open water pelagics we targeted offshore. It was also a chance to put your feet on dry land and explore this strange but oddly beautiful island.

On our last full day before our departure I had one of the crew of the Royal Star ferry me in one of the inflatables ashore, across the reef and onto the beach, just south of Clipperton Rock. I was the only person wanting to fish from the shore that day and, after the dinghy had departed I was quite alone on the island although I could still see the Royal Star anchored some way offshore.

I relished the solitude. After so many days fishing in the company of others it was the first time I had had the chance to be on my own. I've always enjoyed fishing as a solitary sport; one person alone in nature. It is always a time for me to be at one with myself and in harmony with the world about me.

It also gave me the chance to take a look around the island a bit. Now I didn't walk all the way around the place because that's a slog of around six or seven miles and it was a damn hot day. I did however wander about a bit in the South Eastern corner and strolled through the sea bird colonies which was just wonderful. The boobies had young in every stage of development from nearly adult to fluffy little things that looked like animated balls of cotton wool. I wore sandals to protect my feet from the sharp coral sand and doused my bare parts with sun lotion to ward off the fierce rays from the tropical sun. I walked to the edge of the lagoon and looked out across to the far side of the island but I couldn't make out much detail for the place shimmered in the heat.

But mostly, I confess, my attention was captured by the beach and water beyond. I took my fly rod and waded out into the surf to cast, with the prominence of Clipperton Rock behind me. The water was clear as crystal tinged in azure blue. Close to the beach, the water was swarming with Black Trigger Fish, so thick in parts that they bumped against your legs as you

15

waded into the water. These fish would occasionally take a dab at my fly but they mostly graze on the coral and their mouths are too small really to be able to take the big lure type flies I was using. I had other quarry off that beach.

Using a shooting head to my line, I cast as far out as I could over the heads of the hordes of Trigger Fish, stripping my big streamer back towards me. Almost immediately I could see larger fish darting for my lure and turning away with a great flash of silver flanks. In excitement I continued casting, all my attention riveted on the entrancing submarine world between the beach and the outlying reef. Then suddenly a streamlined shape materialised from the left and engulfed my fly with such ferocity that it nearly wrenched my rod from my hands. I lifted the rod to set the hook, as if it was even necessary, the rod arced into an agonised curve and the ratchet on my reel screamed in torment as the fish stripped line away in a heart stopping run towards the reef.

The power in that fish was just boggling and I had no way of stopping that first madcap dash. My heart was in my mouth as the fish ran over the edge of the reef. I could see my line shortly about to be shredded on the sharp edges of coral and my fish away with my lure. Frantically I danced along the beach applying side strain to try and turn the fish's head around. For several nerve racking seconds we were at an impasse but then the fish gave and kited around to the right enabling me to regain some line and play the fish in the relatively open water free of structure on this side of the reef. But it was by no means the end of the battle. That fish fought hard and doggedly, never seeming to tire or weaken. Before long my arm was aching and still the fish battled on. At least I could see it now though; a big beautiful silvered creature twisting and turning on the end of my line.

I don't know how long it took me to subdue that fish but finally I had it at the edge of the surf. I used an old trick of surf angling to beach it by letting a wave carry it onto the beach where it flopped around in shallow water before I could reach down and grasp it by the wrist of the tail, yipping in delight as I secured my prize.

I staggered back up onto the beach grasping my fish and squatted down in the sand to admire it. It was worth admiring for it was beautiful. It must have weighed around twelve or thirteen pounds of compact firm muscle beneath its shimmering silver flanks. It was a Bluefin Trevally: in my opinion one of the loveliest members of the Jack family with its sky-blue fins, mottled blue and green back and silver sides. It was picture perfect; stunning in appearance and shining iridescently in the sunlight. It was also the first one I had ever caught on a fly rod.

It was my intention to release the fish back to the ocean alive. Bluefin Trevally are good to eat although you can sometimes get ciguatera poisoning from them. Still it would have made a fine table fish except for the fact that the dinghy wasn't due to come and pick me up for some hours yet and the fish would have surely spoiled quickly in that hot sunshine. In any case there was a part of me that felt it criminal to kill that beautiful creature and wanted to see it back in the sea to fight another day. After a last look I heaved the fish into my arms and prepared to carry it back into the water to release it. Then somebody spoke behind me!

I swear to God I nearly had a heart attack and damn near dropped that fish in shock. I knew for a fact that I was completely alone on the island. I could still see the ship and both inflatables way out beyond the reef and I'd been able to observe them most of the morning. I was sure nobody else but myself had landed since the dinghy had dropped me off on the beach. Yet that voice behind me was another person on the island.

In shock, I span around and my astonishment increased. There, standing behind me for all the world as if they had sprung up out of the sand, stood a young child. That in itself beggared belief. Naturally there were no children on the Clipperton Exploratory Expedition and no indication whatsoever that there were any other vessels anywhere near us. We hadn't seen another ship for days and, to the best of anyone's knowledge, there had been no settlers on this island for over half a century. So the presence of a young child would have been extraordinary in any circumstances. But there was more to the mystery. This was no ordinary child.

I can only begin to describe the otherworldly feeling that came upon me when I cast eyes on that child. I felt the hair on the back of my neck rise with the strange chill that seemed to shiver through me at the sight. This was the oddest looking child I had ever seen. There was something downright eerie about it; something not of this world; outside my experience.

It is not that the child was hideous or deformed in some way. On the contrary, it appeared to be quite pretty once you got used to its strangeness. I say "it" deliberately because it was actually quite difficult to discern the child's gender. This may sound odd because the child was completely naked and possessed an unmistakable penis. That would appear to decisively indicate that it was a little boy but, and especially in the light of later events, this did nothing to dispel the ambiguity. Had you covered up that one part of the child's anatomy you would have been convinced that it was a girl. It had long oddly formed hair that rose in a crest on the crown but fell in a long cascade down the child's back. The hair was an odd colour too; a sort of silvery blond but with strange greenish streaks in it. The child's features were very feminine. Of course little boys often look quite girly but this child looked every inch a pretty little girl, if a somewhat odd one, if you overlooked the anomaly of its sexual organs.

It wasn't just this indeterminate gender that marked the child out as peculiar however. The most arresting feature in its face was its eyes. They were huge; notably bigger than a normal little boy or girl's and such a vivid colour of blue green that they were quite startling. I'd never seen eyes like that in a person before. They were not unattractive but definitely uncanny. The child's ears were odd as well. They were long and pointed giving the child an almost pixie like look. They were kind of cute really but again I've not seen anybody with pointed ears since I saw "The Lord of the Rings" at the movies.

It's kind of difficult to exactly pin down the curious nature of the child. Reading through what I've just written, it doesn't make the child sound particularly weird. Yet there was something chillingly different about it. I'll kind of stick my neck out here. The kid didn't look human. Now that sounds crazy I know but I can't escape the feeling that this kid wasn't any kind of human I'd ever seen. Oh sure it was basically the right shape for a human if that makes any sense. All the parts were in the right places I guess. But it was still outside of the norm. It didn't seem to correspond to any sort of race of human. It wasn't oriental, Caucasian, African or Amerindian. It didn't seem to correspond to the native Pacific island people you'd see in Tahiti or Hawaii. It was something different; something new.

I guess I must have stared at that child for quite some time so taken aback by its appearance as I was. The kid seemed quite interested in me as well. Or at least that's what I thought. The kid pointed at me and suddenly let out a completely unintelligible babble. Now I'm no linguistic expert. I can manage a few words in Spanish but that's about it. This kid's language however was the most peculiar I'd ever heard. I can't quite explain why. I don't think it would have struck me as strange if the kid had just launched into Mandarin, Polynesian or Swahili or something. I wouldn't have expected to understand those languages but I'd at least have recognised that they were some human language that I was unfamiliar with. The curious rapid fire collection of vocalisations from this child however sounded so alien however, adding to that inhuman aspect of it.

I shook my head and said slowly. "I'm sorry. I don't understand." The kid launched into another burst of that oddly fluid bubbling tongue and pointed again. It was then that I realised that it was not pointing at me but at the fish I was still holding. I blinked in surprise. "You like my fish?" I asked, "You want to touch it maybe?" I held the fish out for the child to touch. It seemed to become quite excited for it reached out and grasped the fish. "Hey there! Be careful!" I warned but I was quite unprepared for what happened next. In a single movement that caught me completely by surprise by its strength, the child wrenched the fish from my grasp. Now that was a big fish for such a small child and a powerful one too but that kid took hold of it with ease. "Hey stop that!" I admonished and made to reclaim my fish.

At this moment I was brought up short by an unearthly menacing screech. I staggered back and looked around wildly for the source of this sound. I saw it soon enough! Racing across the sands towards us was a woman brandishing some weapon that looked like a harpoon. It took far less time than it takes to tell to realise that this woman was mightily pissed and flying to the defence of her child. Her speed was incredible and the hair of her head was literally bristling in agitation. It was also clear that she was of the same ilk as the child; the same alien oddity only more so if anything. It was also clear that she was assuming some danger to her child and quite likely prepared to kill in its defence.

20

I jumped back in alarm. That woman looked mighty dangerous. She leaped between me and her child and hissed in the most terrifying way at me, baring a set of teeth that you never saw on any human before; rows of dagger like dentures. I took a step back and held my hands up in fright. "Hey! I didn't mean any harm. Just talking to the kid. Calm down." She raised that dreadful looking harpoon above her shoulder and for one moment I thought she was going to shish kebab me on it. I don't think I could have done much to stop her either. She looked frighteningly fast and strong and I'm as certain as I can be that I'd have been no match for her.

Up close this woman was even stranger than her curious child. I call her a woman but once again there is some question to her gender. In nearly every respect she was female. She had a lithe female body and prominent breasts. Yet she was nearly as naked as her child bar some strange ornamentation about her waist, bangles on her wrists and ankles and a curious pendant hanging from her neck. Otherwise she wore nothing and, plain to see, she had male and female genitalia. "She" was a hermaphrodite!

Other than that she had all the curious characteristics of her child. The same enormous blue green eyes, the same pointed ears, the same strange hair and that peculiar sense of the unworldly about her. The difference was that she was far less friendly than her child.

For a couple of tension filled seconds I honestly thought she was going to butcher me on the spot. I dropped to my knees in supplication, realising that my life was in the balance. If this strange hermaphrodite considered me a threat to her child she would kill me I was sure. There was a primitive savagery about her outside of the conventions of civilisation.

I think the child saved me. The little one dropped the fish and pulled at its mother's leg. I say "mother" of course with reservations but that's how I interpreted the relationship between them. The kid was babbling away in that unfathomable tongue in some agitation. God knows what it was saying, maybe "Don't hurt the nice man Ma. He gave me his fish." I don't know but "Ma" was in an ill humour and not easily mollified. She turned to the child and hissed at it before treating it to a long monologue in that same curious language. She still seemed pissed but at least her attention was diverted from me.

At least she seemed to calm down a little. She grasped the child by the arm and began to back away cautiously emitting low growls in the back of her throat. The child reached down to pick up the fish once more. "Ma" didn't approve it seemed for she hissed at the child and shook it by the arm. Reluctantly the child dropped it again. I gestured frantically. "Pl... please take it... take it. Have the damn fish. It's yours." I babbled. I gave an expansive gesture with my arms to indicate that she could take the fish.

The woman stared at me for several seconds as if in indecision. Then she gave a low rumble in her chest and hefted her harpoon. I swallowed in sudden fear but my concern was ill placed. Instead of turning the weapon on me she suddenly thrust it down into the body of the fish. It kicked once and then lay still. Then she hefted the fish transfixed on the barbs of her harpoon over her shoulder. She hesitated once more but then she did the strangest thing. She took a bangle from her wrist and flung it on the ground between us and murmured a low growl. I perceived that she expected me to pick it up and cautiously I scuffled forward and took it. It was a series of ornamental seashells and bored pieces of polished stone on a thin sinew. On the face of it, it seemed quite primitive but on closer examination there was some real workmanship in that fashioned bangle and the shells and pebbles were carefully chosen by somebody with an eye for beauty. In astonishment I realised that this was my payment for the fish.

I bowed my head in what I hoped was a gesture of gratitude. "Th... thank you! It's lovely. I... I'll treasure this." I stammered. She seemed satisfied. With a low murmur she turned and, grasping her child began to walk away. I watched the pair of them go with my heart hammering in my breast as they walked off along the beach to the south west. I squatted there for a long time in the sand as they walked off into the distance following the shoreline as it curved around to the west. Finally I remembered my fishing rod and picked it up. When I looked back up I could no longer see them.

It was then that it occurred to me that I was no nearer any sort of explanation as to where this strange woman and her equally strange child had come from. Suddenly I wanted very much to know just where they lived. I laid my rod down and began, nervously, to follow in their footsteps. I peered through the haze ahead to see where they were heading but, to my puzzlement I could see no sign of them. Once I had rounded the south western corner of the island I should have been able to see them. Clipperton island is low lying and has hardly any cover on it. From a slightly higher elevation I should have been able to pick them out unless they were squatting low somewhere. With great caution I picked my way slowly around the island. Then I found their tracks.

This led to the biggest mystery of all. I found their tracks in the sand of the beach quite clearly. They were perfectly fresh and well marked. I followed them until they turned into the soft sand at the shoreline; followed them right down to the water's edge. And there they ended. They went straight into the water and they didn't come out again.

I was baffled. I scoured the sea in front of me for a long time in the hope I would see them swimming. I walked many hundreds of yards up the beach in both directions to see if I could find their tracks emerge once more from the water. I found nothing! For the next three hours I searched assiduously all over the south western flank of that island. There was no sign of them. It was as if they had walked into the water and vanished, literally vanished off the face of the earth.

Somebody later suggested that perhaps they had boarded a small boat at the water's edge. That's nonsense however. I would have seen a boat easily. The sea was flat calm and the Royal Star and both her inflatables were easily visible to the east. There was no boat there. I'd be prepared to swear on it. Those two just vanished into the ocean.

I didn't feel much like fishing after that. In the afternoon one of the ship's crew came to pick me up. I asked if they'd seen any other vessels around the place but they looked at me as if I'd been out in the sun too long. I had much the same reaction from the other anglers aboard the ship over dinner that night as well. I think some thought I was spinning them a yarn. There was a tentative suggestion that I'd fallen asleep on the beach and dreamed the whole thing. On one point everybody was adamant. There were no people on Clipperton Island and there wasn't another ship within hundreds of miles of us.

When I insisted on my story some people suggested that we search the island in case the two people were castaways in need of help. It didn't hold water of course. If they'd been castaways why didn't they signal their hope of rescue to me or anybody else. After all the Royal Star had been anchored off shore for several days and most of us had visited the island in that time. It would have been easy for any castaways to bring themselves to our attention.

I think the ship's skipper felt much the same about it. I think he found my story a little embarrassing and awkward. He seemed in no hurry to investigate it. In any case we were due to sail back for Cabo san Lucas the next morning and nobody wanted to delay our departure for some wild goose chase possibly fuelled by my over excited imagination. To be honest I don't think anybody believed me.

Yet I know what I'd seen. Later that night, after dinner on the Royal Star, the other guys all gathered around in the cabin to drink beer and swap fishing stories. I wanted to be on my own however and I drifted out on deck with a can of beer in my hands. It was dark by then and a night of magic. There was no moon but the sky was ablaze with stars and there was fluorescence in the water around the ship. The milky way was a glorious luminous band across the sky and you could just make out the black shadow of Clipperton Island off our stern to the west. I leaned on the rail with troubling thoughts in my mind. Then the most curious thing happened.

From the direction of the Island and, as far as I could judge, the approximate direction of Clipperton Rock, there came the most eerily haunting sound I have ever heard. It was like a song but no song I ever heard before; the most entrancing and spine tingling wavering ululation you ever came across. For long minutes I listened to that unearthly song, transfixed, almost hypnotised by it. I do not know whether that song had anything to do whatsoever with the strange woman and her child I had met that day but Dr Bloomingdale thought it significant and insisted that I mention it to you.

Suddenly the song ended leaving a deep silence in its wake. It was then that I became aware that I was not alone on the deck. One of the ship's Mexican crew was stood behind me looking strange. "Did you hear that?" I demanded.

He nodded slowly. "Si Senor, I heard it."

"What the hell was it?"

He thought for a moment. "I have heard it before Senor in these waters."

"Then you know what it is."

He shrugged. "Maybe. Perhaps. I don't know Senor. It is not something we talk about." He nodded at me again and turned to walk away "Buenos Noches Senor."

There's not much more to tell you Dr Delmonte. Our voyage home was uneventful and, such was the scepticism of my fellow travellers that I stopped talking about my encounter on the beach at Clipperton Island. If I stopped talking about it, it did not follow that I stopped think about it. That strange day has haunted me ever since. I feel certain in my bones that I saw something remarkable that day; some great mystery that I am at a loss to explain.

In fact I stopped telling people the story some time ago. They just kind of looked at me as if it was one of those fisherman's tall tales. It wasn't until I met Dr Bloomingdale that I recounted it again. I met the Doctor on a trout fishing trip and learned he was marine biologist. We got talking about fishing and fish and marine life in general during the trip and one night we drank a bottle of Bourbon in the lodge we were staying at and I told him about the Clipperton Exploratory Expedition. Well we'd pretty much drunk three quarters of that bottle and I found myself telling him the story I've just recounted to you. He became very interested, excited even and that's when he gave me your address as somebody who has specialised in this field, whatever this "field" might happen to be and urged me to write to you.

What he didn't do was to furnish any particular theory of his own as to the identity of the people I encountered that day and refused to speculate on who they might have been. He did intimate that perhaps you might have experience with these people and might enlighten me as to just what I did see and who I did meet that day. I hope so for the memory of that day has haunted me ever since and that eerie song has visited me in my dreams from this day to that. I know that those were no ordinary people I met then. I feel sure that there is some great mystery behind them; some mystery that might even challenge our very notions of our place in this world. Don't ask me how I know this for I'm at a loss to articulate it. It is just some deep instinct I have. I feel as if I have been privileged to come upon some ancient wonder and to glimpse something that will make me question the very notion of what it means to be human.

I do hope Dr Delmonte that you can help me get to the bottom of this mystery. I await your reply with great eagerness.

Yours faithfully
Stuart Bell."

***

Ngam drew in her breath and laid the letter on the little coffee table knowing that their peaceful interlude was coming to an end. "I guess this means that you'll be on your way again."

Delilah looked agitated and nodded. "Yes. The Lady Shiro is bound for Cabo san Lucas as we speak. They want me to fly out and join the ship."

"Will you be away long?"

Delilah shook her head in indecision. "I don't know honey. It's got to be investigated. It could take a while."

Ngam sighed. "I guess we'd better start packing in the morning then."

Delilah bit her lip and reached into a drawer of the desk. Lying on top of a sheaf of papers was a tiny amber figurine carved into the shape of a woman. It was one of Delilah's most treasured possessions. She never travelled anywhere without it. Fingering the little figurine for comfort, she rose from her desk and strode to the window to stare out through the sleet streaked glass as if seeking out the wild waves of the North Sea beyond. "I'm sorry honey. I have to go."

"Yes I know." murmured Ngam gently. She knew the curious history of her wife. She was one of the very few people who had ever been privileged to read Delilah's private journal; the account of Delilah's adventures long before she had ever met her in a bar in Bankok. She knew the driving passion behind her wife's long studies. Her adventures had left her too many questions. She had spent a lifetime since looking for answers. As she watched Delilah staring out of the window she knew that she had lost her temporarily at least. Her mind was far away; seeking those answers out across the deep blue sea..... and remembering.

Chapter One

From the journal of Dr Delilah Delmonte;

This story has taken me thirty five years to tell and I only finally relate it now in the firm conviction that nobody will believe a single word of it. In many respects that doesn't concern me. I have other motives than those of persuading the reader of the veracity of my tale. I write it more to exorcise a ghost that has haunted me for most of my adult life and will doubtless continue to do so for the rest of my days. It is a story, the memory of which, has been my constant companion these past forty years and has dominated my life in the sense that everything I am today has been shaped by those events in my youth.

My name is Delilah Delmonte or, to be more precise, it is Doctor Delilah Delmonte for I have a doctorate in Greek mythology which, as you will come to see, is deliciously ironic. I'm an old woman now. I'm even a grandmother for heaven's sake. But I was young back then. And what a time it was to be young. I was a teenager in Haight-Asbury, San Francisco during the "Summer of Love" in 1967. I don't remember much about it. I think I was too stoned to know what was happening most of the time. In 1969 I was one of the half a million on Max Yasgur's farm at Woodstock. I was tripping out on acid when somebody told me that Sullivan County had declared a state of emergency and I thought they were talking about me. I stayed on to the bitter end to watch Hendrix's set. The next summer I saw him again on the Isle of Wight in England. There were six hundred thousand of us that time and what time I didn't spend out on the road that year I spent living in a squat in London's Swiss Cottage. The following year I drifted over to mainland Europe. I stayed awhile in a commune in Amsterdam: took too many drugs and slept with too many people in Copenhagen: got raided by the police on a farm in France and avoided being deported by the skin of my teeth. By 1972 I ended up in Greece.

I still have some old faded photographs of myself from those days and I smile now when I look at them. I have a favourite that shows me stood on the Ponte dei Scalzi in Venice taken in 1971. I was a beauty then there is no doubt but I still cringe with amusement at the clothes. I was wearing a full length, flower patterned caftan and the sort of open, leather thonged sandals they used to call "Jesus boots" in London. I had a band around my forehead, bangles on my wrists and ethnic beads and amulets around my neck. In the photo I look every inch a child of my age. God I even had a flower in my long brown hair. I think I fancied myself as some sort of Earth Mother. I had my arm around a handsome looking Italian boy whose hair was nearly as long as mine. I'm damned if I can remember his name. He was an artist, I recall, or at least he was an artist when he wasn't wasted on marijuana and cheap wine. Ah we were young then.

Greece, to begin with, was a great disappointment. It was the one place in Europe that I'd always really wanted to visit. Ever since I was very young I'd been fascinated by the old Greek myths and stories; The Iliad, The Odyssey, the stories of Herakles, Helen of Troy, Jason and the Argonauts, Pandora's box, myths of Atlantis, you name it. One of my favourites (and I just have to laugh at this in retrospect) was the tale of Andromeda, the chained maiden sacrificed to the sea monster Cetus and awaiting the arrival of her hero, Perseus, flying in on his winged steed, Pegasus, to rescue her. I used to lap this stuff up as a kid; reading anything I could about it; even Aesop's fables, anything that could transport to my fantasy world of Ancient Greece. Greece in my mind was this archipelago of sun baked land, islands and deep blue sea populated by jealous competing Gods, tragic maidens and bronzed heroes battling against multi headed serpents, minotaurs and giants or setting sail on perilous quests through seas infested with monsters and treacherous sirens attempting to lure them to their doom; all to win the heart of some maid and at the whim of assorted Gods and Goddesses. I pictured this world of great ruined classical buildings, enchanted olive groves and quaint villages nestled about the rocky shores of a mystical, tranquil sea. It was heady stuff for a small town girl from Iowa.

Nor had my years on the road done anything to dull my idealised image of this Greek fairyland. The culture of my youth was saturated in myth and fantasy. We took marijuana, LSD and magic mushrooms and fancied ourselves connected to some deep vein of ancient wisdom unconnected to the mundane reality of modern life. I'd spent mid-summer's eve at Stonehenge in England and believed that I'd perceived some greater cosmic truth that had nothing to do with the two hundred and fifty micrograms of acid I'd taken and the Grateful Dead tracks we were playing on the portable cassette deck. We'd followed lay-lines; visited the supposed site of Camelot and talked to trees. We believed in Earth Spirits, reincarnation, Chinese fortune telling, astrology and Timothy Leary. The whole world becomes a Magical Mystery Tour with naive, youthful idealism and enough drugs to fuel it. Greece was just to be the culmination of all these dreams; the repository of my most cherished fantasies.

Turning up in Athens, on a miserable February evening, threatened to undermine those long cultivated delusions. For one thing it had never occurred to me that even Greece has a winter of sorts. I just thought the sun shone perpetually there. It was pissing it down with rain in Athens! So much for my sun-drenched olive groves! My Euro-rail card deposited me at Athens' Central

Railway Station (Stathmos Larissis) at about eight o'clock in the evening after what had been almost certainly the dreariest and most miserably uncomfortable railway journey it had ever been my misfortune to experience. It was raining; it was cold and I was quite alone.

I hadn't planned it that way. I'd been telling people for years that it was my ambition to go to Greece and soliciting their participation in the adventure. I had hoped that Dieter, the guy I'd shacked up with in Munich, would come along. But Dieter was a guitar player in a band and they went on tour at about that time. I nearly postponed my Greek trip to go with them. It sounded kind of exciting being on the road with a rock and roll band. In the end it was perhaps a good job that I stuck to my plans. The band got busted trying to sneak half a kilo of hash across the border, hidden in one of their bass speakers and the whole lot of them ended up in jail. Sandy, my English girlfriend, was another that was supposed to accompany me but she'd caught a nasty dose of religion at the Glastonbury Festival the summer before and she'd jetted out to stay in a Buddhist monastery in Nepal instead. Thus I was on my own.

To cap it all I discovered that some asshole had stolen all my traveller's cheques on the train and I turned up in Athens penniless. I spent my first night in Greece trying to sleep in a bus shelter. The next three days were fraught with tension as I wrestled with banks, where hardly anybody spoke English it seemed, trying to recover my lost assets. I had to resort in the end to phoning collect back home and begging my long suffering father to send me some cash. He agreed in the end but only after extracting a solemn promise from me to return home in the summer in time for his and mom's wedding anniversary in June. He'd been trying to get me to come home for years and now he'd finally had my absolute oath to do so. He didn't have to try too hard to obtain it. I was so lonely, homesick and wretched that for the first time in a long time the thought of Iowa and family was suddenly very appealing. I would go home in June. Pa would forward the air plane ticket. I never made that plane. That anniversary was destined to be the most tragic in my parents' marriage.

Chapter Two

Once my financial difficulties were solved I set out to look for the Greek fantasy that was slipping away from me. In Athens it proved elusive. Even back in the seventies Athens was a big, dirty, traffic congested and polluted city. It's worse now, if anything. I went around the usual attractions of Athens. I walked up the Acropolis and took a look at the Parthenon but the place was a tourist trap and full of boorish Germans. I was hampered by the fact that I knew no one, spoke no Greek whatsoever and the tourist authorities seemed more concerned with wealthy visitors than some impoverished, wayward little hippy girl. After a couple of weeks of this I'd had enough and headed for the sea.

To a large extent much of my idealised imagery of Greece was associated with the sea and, particularly, the basin of the Aegean Sea and its myriads of islands. There are over six thousand Greek islands and islets all told, the majority of them in the Aegean. Of those six thousand, there are only about two hundred and twenty inhabited ones and only seventy eight of those have more than a hundred inhabitants on them. You could spend a lifetime exploring all of them. It was now March and I was going home at the beginning of June. I had two months.

Among the islands of the Aegean Sea I began to find the Greece that I had started to think was lost to me. The spring was much kinder than my arrival in Athens and for day after day, week upon week, the sun shone in glory over the magical, azure waters of the Aegean. In the seventies, tourism was just beginning to make its mark on the Aegean islands but most of them remained relatively unsullied by mass commercial exploitation. Among the islands and their people I found an unhurried peaceful existence that seemed little changed in many ways from Homer's day.

Some people had warned me that many of the islanders were very conservative and unlikely to welcome some hippy girl of the sex and drugs and rock and roll generation amidst them. In fact, for the most part, I was nearly everywhere treated with the warmest hospitality imaginable. I was often the only visitor to an island and I suppose there was always that air of a little lost waif about me that endeared me to the local people. Whatever the reason, they took me under their wings. There were some places I stayed where the locals were literally squabbling among themselves for the honour of putting me up in their houses. One island I was on the locals threw a fiesta in my honour on the night before my departure and the whole village turned out to see me off the next day.

It was most welcome this hospitality because one of the major problems I faced was an ongoing battle with the infuriatingly haphazard schedule of the ferries that shuttled around the islands. The ship would drop you on one island and, after seeing all there was to see in an afternoon, you found that the next ship wasn't due for week and that's if the damn thing bothered to arrive at all. Helen's face might have launched a thousand ships but you can bet your last dime that not one of the bastards turned up on time. On top of that, the ships themselves were as motley a collection of rusting, derelict death traps as it would be possible to imagine. I'd have rather travelled on the Argo half the time.

Truthfully though, I suffered these inconveniences gladly for it was an idyllic time, my passage through the Aegean islands. Not only did I benefit from the hospitality of the natives I also found myself relatively well off. Away from the tourist traps of Athens, Greece, in those days, was ridiculously cheap. I could eat out in a cafe or restaurant for a dollar fifty and get blind drunk for two. Even the ferry prices were reasonable. The vagaries of the ferries even suited me to some extent for I was in no real hurry to get anywhere in particular. I just kind of aimlessly wandered around, washing up like a piece of flotsam on whatever island the next ship happened to be going to. It suited me just dandy.

One thing I won't tell you in this story are all the names of the various islands I happened upon. For one thing I can't remember half of them and secondly I have my reasons for concealing the identity of those places that came to be of the most significant in this tale. I decided on this policy of secrecy long ago and I've stuck to it ever since. Not even to those few people that I have, in confidence, related the salient facts of this story previously have I revealed the exact geographical location where it took place. Some of those in possession of the broad outline of events that overtook me in that journey may well be able to piece together a rough idea of where I spent the summer of '72 but most of those are either sworn to secrecy, not fully informed of the precise details of my story or dead. I have my reasons for this deliberate obfuscation and they are altruistic reasons for a higher purpose than those of my own personal dignity or reputation. I truly believed, back then, that it was important to hide the truth and, in so doing, protect the inhabitants from the destructive influence of human investigation. Those reasons have somewhat lessened in later years but I still hesitate to fully reveal those facts lest I bring a great evil upon an ancient and wondrous mystery of our world.

Thus I must beg the reader's forgiveness if my geography is deliberately vague and ask them to understand that I have only the best intentions in being so.

Oh I will mention a couple of the places I visited since they are fully on the tourist map now and they are quite revealing of the sort of wandering I was indulging in. I spent three days on Mykonos for example. These days Mykonos is a horribly spoiled tourist destination but it was a beautiful and charming place back then; an impossibly picturesque island of some thirty three square miles of quaint white washed villages crammed with tiny narrow paved streets nestled around clear blue bays and inlets, white sand beaches and the characteristic ancient, squat little, windmills that dot the hillsides around the island. Even then though, the first waves of new tourists were beginning to make their impact on the place. I was quite interested in these tourists to begin with because they seemed to consist largely of attractive young men. I spent three days naively trying to hit on them until it finally dawned on me that Mykonos was turning was turning into the tourist destination of choice for the cognoscenti among European gay men. I gave it up and made my way to Lesbos instead.

Before you ask, yes Lesbos did have some ulterior significance to me other than as another beautiful Greek island. I was a child of the love generation remember and every bit as likely, in those days, to jump into bed with another girl as I was with a man. (not that my willingness has altered over the years; I just have less opportunities at my age now.) Actually Lesbos didn't endear itself to me. Oh it's a pretty place right enough and at six hundred and thirty square miles in size it's the third largest Greek island, set just off the Turkish coast in the Eastern Aegean. I guess the reason I didn't much take to it was that it was one of the few places among the islands where I encountered less than warm hospitality. Lesbians (and I use the term here in its demographic meaning to denote an inhabitant of the island of Lesbos) were less than amused by the fact that the title of their collective identity had been appropriated by gay women and disinclined to be welcoming to a young woman of presumably ambiguous sexuality turning up on their island and flaunting the fact in their faces. I hung around for a couple of days, bought a slim translation of

Sappho's poems and caught the next boat out of there.

Otherwise my ramblings were largely random and unplanned; just a journey through a bewitching seascape of impossibly blue water liberally sprinkled with exquisite islands of captivating beauty. I fell in love with Greece all over again. I was as happy as I'd ever been and if my idle wandering seemed of little purpose or reason it was enough then to be young, alive and in harmony with the world about me.

But I was running out of time. March came and went. April passed too in hazy days of balmy sunshine and, before I knew it, it was May. I was due to fly home at the end of the month and I reckoned I had but two weeks left of my Aegean idyll before I'd have to make my way back to the mainland and begin my preparations to fly home to Iowa. I set off for one last adventure to a group of islands I hadn't visited yet on yet another rickety old ship. Somewhere, en route to that destination, in the middle of the Aegean Sea, I contrived to fall overboard.

Chapter Three

Over the years I've told the story of how I managed to fall off a ship in the Aegean Sea in a number of imaginative ways. I apologise in advance therefore to all the people that know me and to whom I have related these edited and fictitious accounts. I've told that I tripped over some equipment, carelessly left by the deckhands, that precipitated my going over the rail. I've told others that I was caught by surprise by a sudden lurch from the ship that threw me through a gap in the rail and even to others yet that a rusted section of the rail gave way under my weight and dropped me into the sea. I think I've told some that it was a combination of all three things. I'm afraid it was none of these things and, since this is an account of the truth, I will tell that truth even though it reflects badly on me. The truth is that I was drunk on cheap ouzo and high as a kite on Moroccan hash I'd bought off a guy a week before.

It was evening and I'd gone out onto the after deck to watch the sun set. I was barely dressed. All I wore was a floral patterned sari wrapped about me and quite naked underneath but I was alone on the after deck and cared not. The sun was setting in radiant fire in the west and turning the sea into a metallic sheen of molten copper. I had no idea where we were. I have a vague recollection of some tiny slivers of land far to the east. Feeling elevated by the glorious spectacle of the sunset I did something inordinately foolish. I climbed onto the middle bar of the guard rail and, exalting in the breeze in my hair, I spread my arms wide, fancying myself to appear like some Greek Goddess throwing her arms wide in benediction over the scene before me. Inevitably I lost my balance, fell forward and went straight over the stern of the ship.

You may take it from me that there is no better a

combination than that of chill water and mortal danger to induce instant sobriety. I came spluttering to the surface, being tossed around in the white water being churned from under the ship's stern by the screws, and yelled in panic for help. My cries went unheeded and the ship growled and rattled its way inexorably into the distance. The ship hadn't seemed to be travelling very fast while I was aboard but it appeared to be disappearing alarmingly rapidly now. I yelled and yelled and yelled but I knew it was futile. In those dreadful moments several realisations came to me in dreadful certainty: it was almost certain that nobody had seen me go over the side of the ship, the nearest land was miles away, I was an indifferent swimmer in any case and that I was surely going to die.

You think you're going to live forever at that age. Your own mortality seems unthinkable until it suddenly rears up and stares you in the face. As the disturbed water of the ship's passage evened out and calmed I cried. The ship was now a speck in the distance and, as I bobbed alone in the darkening water as the sun set, I cried in fear and grief; grief for my young life, full of promise, that I had thrown away in a moment of foolishness.

What does a young girl think about when faced with certain death? I think it was Samuel Johnson who coined the phrase that it concentrates a man's mind wonderfully knowing he is to be hanged in the morning. Well the same goes for frightened little girls bobbing about in the Aegean Sea. I thought of my ill spent days of the past few years; too many drugs and too much alcohol. I thought of my family back in Iowa who loved me and despaired of my dissolute life. I wanted so desperately to run to them now, beg their forgiveness and tell them I loved them. I wanted my father's calm wisdom and my mother's gentle compassion. But it was too late. I would never see them again. I think I prayed. The last sliver of the sun dipped below the horizon and I knew I would not live to see it rise again; the fall of night mirroring the darkness closing on my existence.

I thought perhaps that I should end it quickly; allow myself to sink and get it over with. I'd read somewhere that drowning was supposed to be an easy way to die. But life is nothing if not stubborn and some tenacious inner resilience refused, as yet, to so quickly abandon my life.

I shivered in the water. Even the Aegean Sea can be cold in May. Then there was a splash in the water behind me. I whipped my head around in fear to see only the disturbance made presumably by some large creature from the depths below. My first thought was of sharks. I'd been contemplating the relatively peaceful death by drowning. Being eaten by sharks was another matter entirely. I felt a cold tingle of dread run the length of my spine. Something touched my leg and I screamed involuntarily in panic. There was another splash and the creature emerged at the surface at few feet away and I stared in stunned disbelief. It was a person's head!

Of all the most incredible miracles I could have thought of it was the realisation that there was somebody else in the water beside me in that vast expanse of sea. It was getting dark and I could make little of my companion's features but I tried to gasp a greeting. There was no response. Like quicksilver the figure darted back beneath the surface. I cast my head about wildly trying to see them again but they had vanished. Where had they come from? What where they doing in the water so far out to sea? For a few seconds I began to think I had imagined them; that they were some hallucination born of my addled brain and desperation. Then suddenly they came back up behind me and grasped me about the chest gripping me beneath my arms. Incredibly I felt warm naked flesh against me and breasts against my back. It was a woman. Then she kicked with her legs and she was propelling me backwards through the water.

That girl could *swim*! I could feel the immense power in her limbs and she dragged me through the water as effortlessly as a rag doll. I couldn't have made better pace on my own. I was content to lay inert and let her pull me along; suddenly feeling immensely safe in her strong arms. There seemed to be some purpose to her swimming too. She set a course and followed it doggedly heading for I knew not where.

If she could swim, it seemed that conversation was not her strong suit. I tried to babble out some thanks but received only grunts in reply. I supposed she must be saving her breath for the effort of keeping me afloat and pulling me through the water so I held my peace. As darkness fell the girl propelled us both relentlessly though the water towards some destination I could only conjecture at.

I have only the most disjointed memories of that long swim. I think I must have been slipping in and out of consciousness and delirium. I know that on occasions she relinquished her grip on me but stayed close by to keep me afloat. I think she was just taking a rest before turning once more to the labour of hauling me through the water. She needed to rest certainly because she must have pulled me many miles throughout that long strange night. It was an incredible achievement and even now I can still wonder at the magnitude of it. Of course I didn't know then that there was nobody else quite as well suited to the requirements of that task. It just seemed miraculous at the time. God she was strong and, whatever may have happened later, I still know that owe that girl my life. With inexorable determination she pulled that lost girl in the sea through the darkness to safety.

It took all night. I don't actually recall making landfall. I guess I must have been pretty far gone by then. My first memory of it was in waking up stretched out on some sand and feeling the warmth of the morning sunshine on my back. I remember choking up a lot of water so I guess I must have swallowed quite a bit throughout that long swim. As my eyes came slowly into focus the first thing I saw seemed so bizarre and absurdly incongruous that, for several seconds, I could only lie there, blinking at it foolishly. It was a battered old, enamelled sauce pan sat on the sand two feet away from my head. In confusion I eased up on my elbows to look at it more closely. It was half full of clear water. Tentatively I dipped a finger in the water and tasted it. Gloriously it was fresh water. I was parched and eagerly I snatched the pan up in both hands and drank deeply from it. I heard a noise from behind me and whipped around in surprise. The girl was sat on a rock ten yards away watching me carefully.

Somehow I staggered to my feet, perceiving as I did that I was on the beach of a tiny cove surrounded by rocks. I hadn't managed to see, with any clarity, my saviour during the long night of our swim but now I saw her clearly, by the light of day, and I felt the hair on the back of my neck rise as a sudden, unearthly chill of fear came over me. For this was no ordinary woman squatting on that rock. I can still feel that eerie sensation I had when I first saw her as if it was yesterday; that instant recognition that I was looking at somebody that fell outside of my experience of humankind. There was an unworldly quality about her and something old and ancient as if the sight of her stirred some forgotten, archaic, ancestral memory buried in my consciousness.

She was sitting with her knees drawn up to her chin and gazing at me fixedly with her eyes; those incredible eyes. She was quite naked bar a sort of belt fashioned about her waist, some odd beads and seashells braided into her hair and a curious amulet on a thong about her neck. Her skin seemed pale and translucent and her hair was silver. By silver I don't mean the faded grey of the old lady or even the hue we call platinum blond. Her hair literally had the metallic sheen of polished silver and it grew strangely too. It fell down her back in a long mane but on the top of her head it stood up like the kind of hairstyles punk rockers affected in the eighties. I was later to learn that that hair of hers was actually mobile and a good indicator of her mood. When she was relaxed and tranquil her hair would lie flat on the top of her head but when she was wired, tense or, as she was at this moment, just intensely curious and excited it would bristle up.

Her ears were extraordinary and they came in time to be one of my favourite features about her. They were long and pointed like Mr Spock's from Star Trek only more delicate and elegant. Ever since I'd been a child I'd always wanted to have pointy ears like a pixie's. Well this girl had them and I found them unbearably cute. They were animated too and she constantly twitched them, especially when she was excited. When she was sad they appeared to droop.

Her nose was another expressive part of her features. It was turned up and slightly flattened and it was always twitching and sniffing the air about her. I came to recognise that she had an acute sense of smell and the scent of things was important to her. There was a territorial and possessive function to her sense of smell I was to discover in time for she marked her ground and her possessions with her scent including, and most particularly, me. But I'm getting ahead myself now.

The single most arresting features on her face were her eyes and these were truly remarkable. I had never seen such enormous eyes on a person. They were great expressive globes framed under exaggeratedly high arched eyebrows. And the colour of them! The irises were a startling and penetrating emerald green.

Whenever she stared directly at you, which was often I might add, they were like great big laser beams boring into you. They were another thing that changed with her mood. If she was angry or tense they were like steely green flints but they became almost misty when she was wistful or contented.

As to the rest of her body it was shapely and womanly but with well-defined muscles. Even had I not had the evidence of her efforts in swimming so far to bring me here to safety to go on I would have seen immediately that she was immensely strong. Her breasts were high and firm and I noticed no anomalies there although I was to learn in time that even they were possessed of their idiosyncrasies. She seemed to have very long legs and her feet were broad and sturdy looking. Her hands on the other hand were long and immensely tactile with long probing fingers. There was something odd about her hands and I didn't understand what it was until I took a closer look. There was webbing between the fingers on her hands and the pattern was repeated on her feet.

Looking back over the brief description I've penned it may seem as if the girl I've described was perhaps rather unusual but by no means so far out of the ordinary. It's very hard to convey that otherworldliness about her convincingly. Any one of her curious features alone might have been dismissed as a curiosity of hers but all of them together were strikingly strange. You just knew by looking at her, sat on her rock staring at you with her hair, nostrils and ears quivering in suppressed excitement, that you were looking at a person quite unlike any you had ever met before in your life. It was uncanny, disturbing and oddly frightening and, at that point, I hadn't even seen some of the oddest features of her anatomy.

It was nearly impossible to tell how old she was. Superficially she seemed to have the body of a young woman no older than I was myself but there was that odd feeling of having no reference point to age her by. In fact, throughout the time I knew her, I never came to any satisfactory conclusion about her age. At times you had the feeling she was a sage and ancient woman but she could just as easily appear to be an excited or petulant child. You had the feeling that all your usual indicators regarding a person's age had no relevance here. She might have been a precocious child or she might have been a thousand years old for all you knew. She didn't fit into the mould or fall along the normal time lines of your experience.

I suppose I must have stood and stared at her for several seconds, so profound an impact did she have on me, before I remembered my manners. After all, for all her eerie oddity, this girl had saved my life and it was downright rude not to express my gratitude for that. I hadn't exactly picked up fluent Greek on my travels but at least I had learned the words for hello and thank you. Well I tried them hesitantly on her but she just looked at me oddly without replying and showed not the slightest indication that she had understood a word I had said. More in hope than anything I tried her with English. Oddly this seemed to elicit some sort of reaction. She rocked back and forth on her rock and her ears twitched furiously. An odd unfathomable smile seemed to form on her face and a curious low growling purr seemed to come from the back of her throat; a sound I was later to recognise as a signal of her pleasure. Again I am certain that she hadn't a clue what I was saying. She just liked hearing me talk.

With communications at an impasse I just kind of stood there flummoxed. I wondered briefly if she was perhaps simple and couldn't talk at all, for the only vocalisations I'd heard from her were grunts, snorts and that odd purring sound. No sooner had the notion occurred to me, however, than she suddenly, and without warning, gave voice to a long monologue. Well that settled one thing. She didn't speak Greek. I'd heard enough of that language to recognise it by now and this was most certainly not it. In fact I'd never heard a language like it and forty years later I still haven't heard the like again. It was the oddest fluid outpouring, rising and lowering in pitch and tone; extraordinarily melodious yet containing strange gurgling sounds and guttural notes. It ranged from sweet high tones to low soft growls, constantly shifting and changing from fast staccato patterns to slow harmonious phrases. You got the feeling that if water in the sea or a bubbling stream could talk that would have been the language it would have used. It was entrancing to listen to and completely incomprehensible.

It was a language too and not just random vocalisations. There was meaning and significance in it. In time I got to be able to be able to recognise them. I can't say that I ever came to understand it much less ever speak it. I don't know if it would have even been possible, with my vocal organs, to speak in that tongue. Nevertheless I did, in time, begin to pick out meanings from it and begin to grasp some of the richness of it. God how I wish I could have had a tape recorder then to preserve that speech for posterity. I have made a study of language these past forty years and I am as certain as I can be that her language belonged to no linguistic family that I've ever come upon since. Even languages as diverse as English, Greek, German and French all belong to the same family and have their common roots in the Indo-European phylum of languages that dominate all of Europe, the Iranian plateau and South Asia. This was something entirely different. Had I been able to record it then I might have been the only person to have committed that tongue to the archives of human knowledge.

Having delivered her speech the girl suddenly

snaked off her rock. I do not use the expression lightly. There was something almost reptilian about the way she suddenly uncoiled from her seating position to a stance in front of me. It was part of the strangeness about her those sudden fluid motions; so quick and yet so controlled and graceful. But that was not the thing that arrested my attention just then.

While she had been hunched on her rock her private parts had been concealed from me. (not that she had any "private" parts of course because she never wore clothes). Now she was stood in front of me I was afforded a view of her groin and I recoiled in shock. She had no pubic hair whatever and, hanging between her legs, was a large and all too noticeable penis.

I stood rooted to the spot not knowing how to react. Until that moment there might have been many oddities about her but there had been nothing whatever to suggest that she was anything but female. She had in fact, in spite of her more curious features, the body of a young attractive woman. That single grotesque anomaly seemed ludicrously incongruous when set upon her female form. It wasn't just a small anomaly either. Many a man who fancied himself a stud would have been proud to own the organ dangling so bizarrely from this girl's loins.

In some ways I found this the most shocking aspect of her yet. In my defence I must point out that this was 1972. In those days the issues of transgendered people were still largely unknown and taboo. The Stonewall riots had only occurred in 1969 and even the gay rights movement was still in its infancy. Across most of mainstream America homosexuality was still largely considered a mental illness at best and a disgusting, criminal perversity at worst. Transgendered people were still well off the radar. If we thought of them at all it was in terms of sad lonely perverts putting on women's clothes in their homes or drag queens in sleazy gay bars.

Even today, with our thankfully far greater understanding and tolerance for the diversity of human sexuality and gender, many people are still uncomfortable with the whole idea and transgendered people are among the most widely discriminated against people in society. Back then it must have been horrible for them. Even I, who considered myself to be tolerant and after all of sufficient sexual ambiguity myself as to be considered bi-sexual, was taken aback to see somebody so clearly cross the boundary of gender identity we had always so fondly believed to be fixed and immutable.

When I could tear my eyes away from her sexual organs I noticed that she was tall. She was probably about six feet tall which put her well above me because I just about made a shade over five foot one. I was just a little slip of a thing. This girl towered over me. I saw the muscles rippling in her long legs and understood a little of the power in them that had driven us so many miles through the night.

She stalked up to me slowly. She seemed animated and excited. Her ears were quivering beguilingly; her nostrils twitching and sniffing as if trying to catch the scent of me. Her eyes were dancing all over me and I felt suddenly shy before their searching appraisal. My sari hadn't been improved by a night of immersion in the Aegean Sea but I pulled it about myself protectively under her gaze. Nobody had told this girl that it was rude to stare when she was little it seemed. Curiously, she began to walk in circles around me, examining me from different angles and emitting that odd little purring sound in her throat as she did so. Her walk became quicker and more agitated as she circled me and I felt more and more afraid. Then suddenly, in a lightning fast and fluid motion, she darted up and grasped the material of my sari, ripping it away from me so quickly that I was powerless to prevent it.

I squealed in alarm and tried to cover my nakedness with my hands. She flung the remnants of my sari aside carelessly and recommenced her circling of me. She seemed more excited than ever. Her hair was bristling on her head alarmingly. She seemed even stranger now as well for, so close to her I could detect other features about her which further persuaded me of the girl's particular singularity. Her hair for instance didn't just grow on her head. A slim mane of it actually extended down over her neck and down her back to just below her shoulder blades, following the line of a curious raised ridge that extended the length of her spine. Running too from the base of her neck and between her shoulder blades were two odd flaps of skin overlaying her shoulders. These were the oddest thing and quite clearly regular on both sides of her shoulders and the coverings of two openings into her body. I had no idea what they were although I later came to a conclusion about them. In the time as I came to know her they were not easy things to examine closely for she disliked being touched there and would slap my hand away if I tried. Nevertheless as I came to observe her on a daily basis their function became obvious. I'm going to stick my neck out here. They were the coverings to her gills.

At last she seemed to have seen enough and came to stand a few feet in front of me. Then she grinned and I swear I nearly fainted. Her teeth were two rows of curved and bluntly pointed daggers. She growled softly in her throat and, God help me, I thought she was going to EAT me! Then she growled more urgently and her true intention became startlingly obvious. Her penis (forgive me for that bizarre sounding personal pronoun but I could never think of her as anything but feminine) was fully erect. It was a horrifying sight. To my fevered eyes it looked gargantuan; a great quivering organ thrusting out from her loins with single-minded, malevolent intent and, as her eyes glittered with excited purpose, I knew instantly, exactly what she intended to do with it.

I squealed in panic, turned and ran; racing over the sand of that little beach towards the rocks beyond. In terror I glanced back over my shoulder as I reached the rocks. She was stalking after me with that unearthly grin on her face and that monstrous erection preceding her like the Sword of Damocles. Sobbing with fear I dashed inland. There was a scrubby rocky knoll and I scrambled up it seeking the summit. I'm not quite sure what I intended to do there. I think I had some notion about seeing if I could spy somebody from the top who could respond to my cries for help.

The view from the summit offered no comfort though. Instead it drove me to despair. It had always been a pretty fair bet that I was on an island. I had had no idea, however, that it was such a small one. I could see the whole thing from the summit of that knoll. It could not have been more than six or seven hundred yards wide at its widest point; just a few acres of rocky scrub and, even from the most superficial observation, quite obviously uninhabited apart from myself and that frightening creature now beginning to slowly climb the knoll behind me. In panic I looked around for refuge. I could see a depression in the centre of the island and there the only trees of the island grew; a sad little group of gnarled olives close by the ruins of an ancient villa that showed at least that somebody had once lived here. I fled from the top of the knoll, scrambling through the scrub whose thorns caught at my naked flesh and across the rocky ground, which hurt my bare feet, making for that copse of trees and the ruined villa, seeking some place to hide.

She was still stalking me patiently. I could hear snatches of what sounded like some eerie song coming from her throat. I realised later that she could have caught me easily at any time she wished. She was not only taller and stronger than I she was also a hell of a lot faster. It would have been simplicity itself for her to overtake me. She was just taking the time to relish her pursuit; her excitement increasing with the chase. She was playing with me.

The olive grove and the ruined villa held no sanctuary. Even if there had been some hiding place she would have sniffed me out in no time. I later learned that her sense of smell was so acute that she could track me down anywhere by scent alone. Nor did there seem much mileage in climbing a tree to evade her. The olive trees were a pretty stunted little lot and I had no reason to assume that she was any less arboreal than I was in any case. As she appeared at the edge of the olive grove I turned and bolted for the shore line. I was on the far side of the island by now and there was another little beach there. I dashed down it to the water's edge. God only knows what I intended to do. Did I have some fool notion about jumping into the water and trying to swim away? If I'd stopped for a moment to think I must have surely realised how futile that would have been. This woman could have creamed any Olympic standard swimmer on the planet. You do the craziest things when you're fleeing in panic.

My evasive schemes were academic in any case, for, before I reached the water she abandoned her slow stalking and suddenly exploded into a blur of motion and caught me by my hair in her fist. I screamed and tried to beat her arm away with my hands but she ignored my feeble flailing and turned to drag me by my hair back up the beach. I struggled but the agonising pull on my hair was relentless and I stumbled after her. In a little corner among some rocks she turned, without relinquishing her grip on my hair, and looked at me. I was squealing and gibbering hysterically and pulling at her arm trying to dislodge its hold on my hair. In one of those terrifyingly fast movements of hers she raised her free hand and slapped me hard across the face.

The sudden stinging blow to my face shocked me into silence. She hissed at me. I swear this is the truth. She hissed at me like a snake and parted her lips to expose her teeth. I cowered in terror and she treated me to another monologue of her incomprehensible speech before twisting her fist in my hair and forcing me to my knees; her eyes blazing in green fire. I grovelled on the sand before her; pleading with her not to hurt me. She regarded me thoughtfully, it seemed, for a few seconds and then dropped to squat in the sand beside me. She opened her mouth and leaned toward me. I recoiled with a squeak of fear thinking that she was going to bite me.

Instead she did the most curious thing. She put out her tongue and licked me on the side of my face. Her tongue seemed incredibly long and mobile, and its surface was rough and rasped like a cat's. She rolled her tongue around in her mouth as if savouring the taste of me and gave a little purr of contentment. Evidently she liked the taste. Then she took a firm hold of me and began to explore my body with her hands and her tongue. It was not the slightest use in resisting her. She was terrifyingly strong. She held me immobile as she rasped her tongue all across my face, purring softly as she did so and pausing occasionally to twitch her nostrils and take a deep draught of my scent. She even wriggled her tongue into my ears and I cringed at the tickling sensation of the curiously hard end of it squirming in my ear. She took a firm hold on my face and forced my mouth open to probe inside with her tongue. It was not by any stretch of imagination a kiss. She was just exploring the inside of my mouth and tasting my saliva.

She grasped my wrists together firmly in one hand and then began to run her tongue over my body. She licked my neck and shoulders, raised my arms to lap away in my armpit and grasped my breast with her free hand and ran her tongue over it, the rough surface chafing at my nipple. There was no sense of seduction in this action of licking me. It was almost as if she was grooming me or just taking pleasure in the flavour of my skin. And she couldn't seem to get enough of the smell of me for she sniffed every part of my body with intense concentration. I had stopped struggling by now. I just squatted there inertly as if hypnotised, staring at her in horrified silence and feeling her tongue rasp against my flesh. She was touching me with her fingers too, probing every inch of my body; squeezing, kneading and stroking as if to extract the maximum tactile sensation from the feel of me.

Inevitably her probing fingers found my sex and I started violently as I felt her touch me there. She shook me roughly with a low growl and taking a firmer grip she began to explore my sex with her fingers. I bit my lip to choke back a whimper as I felt a long, tactile finger worm its way into my vagina. She wriggled her finger about inside experimentally for a second or two and then withdrew it. She lifted her finger to her face and took a deep breath of the smell of it. Her hair rippled in delight at the scent of it and she gave a low deep purr of satisfaction. Her eyes seemed to grow misty as she put out her tongue and licked her finger to savour the taste of my sex. It appeared to whet her appetite for she gazed down meaningfully at my groin.

Almost instantly I knew what she wanted to do and I began to struggle again. But her excitement was growing and, without warning, she upended me and laid me flat on my back on the sand. She grasped my ankles and drew my legs up over my body to a point where my knees were near my ears. Then she swung her legs over mine trapping my calves under her knees facing toward my rear and pinioning my arms with her legs. I think I've seen wrestlers pin a person in this fashion and doubtless there is some technical name for the hold. For all practical purposes though it meant that my rear was raised in the air and my exposed sex lay completely at her mercy inches away from her face.

From my prone position beneath her rump I had the unwelcome opportunity to observe her own sexual organs at close quarters. What I saw shocked me even more. I hope the reader will forgive me for the following graphic details I am about to describe but this is important for an understanding of this woman and there really is no way of telling this delicately. This creature who was so delightedly abusing me was possessed not only of a large and prominent penis but also an obviously swollen and glistening vagina too. She was a hermaphrodite. Oddly there was no scrotal sac but there were a pair of swellings under the skin which I was later to conclude corresponded to her testes. The darker folded skin which should have formed the scrotum instead became the labia majora surrounding her vagina. Nor, I noted, was her penis simply an enlarged clitoris as might have been expected in a person with ambiguous genitalia for there seemed to be a quite separate clitoris. In fact her female and male genitalia seemed almost completely separate from each other. Even in the impossible situation I was in I still found time to wonder where exactly she peed from. It was a mystery I was never to solve by the way. She always went out into the sea to rid herself of bodily wastes.

One thing was certain; her sexual organs had quite separate sources of fluid lubrication. Her vagina was dripping wet with her excitement. I say dripping not as a mere turn of phrase. It was quite literally dripping. I could feel drops of fluid falling on my face. It was not alone either for there were drops of liquid seeping from the head of her penis as well. I could feel them landing on my breasts. I felt my head reeling with the implications of this dual sexuality of hers. Could it be really possible that she could function biologically as both male and female? Was it possible, God forbid, that she could even impregnate herself?

Even as I stared in horror at her sexual organs she was obviously entranced by mine. She took a long deep smell of my sex and then, parting the lips bent to lick it. Her purring became almost a low rumbling growl as she lapped at my sex, for all the world, like a cat lapping a saucer of milk. I lay helplessly pinned beneath her whimpering softly in humiliation as she licked away there obviously relishing every taste of my private sanctum. She seemed intent upon extracting every last morsel of my juices from me on her tongue, even penetrating my vagina with her long tongue to wriggle it about inside me. She became ever more excited by her tasting too for, to my shame and in spite of my bizarre situation, my body reacted involuntarily to the stimulation of her tongue and my sex produced fluid of its own which she lapped up eagerly, clearly enjoying the flavour of it.

There is one thing I haven't mentioned and I should do for it is important. Ever since I had come into close contact with this girl I had become aware of her scent. In fact it was strong and unavoidable. This is not to say that it was unpleasant. On the contrary it was quite a pleasant, if somewhat strange, and evocative aroma. It was very difficult to pin down exactly what it smelled of though, although it did spark some odd feeling of having come upon it before even if exactly where proved elusive to the memory. It was the scent that I would always associate with her but for many years I failed to find its equivalent. Finally I did find something very like it. She smelled, in fact, very like ambergris. Ambergris, for those unfamiliar with it, is a curious substance, found floating in the oceans, that is the partially digested remnants of the beaks of Giant Squid which have been vomited up from the stomachs of Sperm Whales. Put like that it sounds horrible but in fact ambergris is a rare and valuable substance. In the days when whaling was allowed it was one of the most valuable products from Sperm Whale carcasses. It's used as an ingredient and fixative agent in expensive perfumes. This girl smelled like that and the parts of her from which she smelled most strongly of it were her sexual organs.

Finally she ceased her probing of my sex with her tongue and jumped aside releasing me. I scrambled to my knees and regarded her warily. Oddly she seemed to have changed colour. When I had first seen her, her skin had been very pale. Now it was much darker as if she had spent a day or two sunbathing. It was another of her oddities that I would recognise in time. When fresh from the sea she would always appear pale but just a short time in the sun and her skin would darken as if her body produced natural colouration quickly to protect her from the sun. I suppose it's the same process as a body tanning in ultra-violet light but it was much faster and ephemeral.

But this was not the thing that most impressed me as I looked at her fearfully. Her excitement was clearly reaching a fever. She was giving vent to a continuous low growling and her penis, that monstrous penis, was literally quivering and twitching, fluid seeping from its tip, as she stared fixedly at my sex. I think I had just time to mouth "Please no!" before she grasped me and spun me around on my knees. She was behind me and she gripped my hips tightly. I squealed in alarm as I felt the head of that dreadful penis questing urgently at the opening of my vagina. I tried desperately to squirm away but she gripped me tighter and punished my wriggling with a hard slap on my rump. Then, with a grunt of satisfaction, she impaled me on that frightful organ, driving it inexorably into me until I thought I would split asunder with its violation of me.

Once she had buried that terrible thing in me to the

hilt, she began to thrust at me urgently. I never would have thought that it was even physically possible for me to take the full length of that thick penis into my body. It was as if somebody had forced their fist and their arm deep into me. Yet it was not some inert object upon which I was now skewered. It felt like something alive inside me like some strange thick snake squirming deep into my vagina. It seemed to have concentric ridges around it like raised knobbly rings and I could feel it literally pulsating within me.

She was not what you might have described as gentle with me. I can remember shrieking in pain and humiliation, digging my nails into the sand, as she violated me, her urgency increasing as her hips slapped hard against my backside with her thrusts. She was growling alarmingly and the violence of her thrusts became such that she was literally lifting me off my knees and pushing me along the sand. I was sobbing in anguish and pleading with her but if she even understood my distress she ignored it under the imperatives of her need. For a second time my body betrayed me for I felt a rising arousal in my loins at her thrusting. In some way this was the most terrible thing of all that my treacherous body could so react to this unspeakable violation of it. I whimpered in shame and prayed for deliverance.

Then the growling in her throat turned to a high keening wail as she rammed her engorged organ into me to its maximum penetration and abandoned herself to orgasm. I could feel her distended member pulsing violently within me and I thought it would never stop as it pumped its ejaculation deep into me, flooding my womb with her seminal fluid. This latter may seem fanciful but it is anything but. How much semen does a man ejaculate on orgasm... a tablespoonful... two perhaps? Well from my observations (and I assure you that, over the coming days, I had all too many opportunities to observe it) her average ejaculation would have filled a half pint mug generously. There seemed no end to it. You wondered where it was all coming from.

That fearful climax seemed to have spent her for she half collapsed against me; breathing heavily with odd wheezing notes and purring softly in her throat. Then, mercifully, she withdrew that awful thing from me. It was like pulling the stopper from a bottle of soda you have shaken too much for, as she withdrew, her semen gushed from my vagina and poured down my thighs. She squatted back on her heels purring to herself and I collapsed on my side weeping piteously.

She regarded the semen pouring from my sex interestedly for a second or two. Then she wriggled up to me and began to scoop it up with her fingers. She tasted it with satisfaction on her tongue and I thought that she was going to lick it all up. Instead she began to smear it all over my body; across my back, my belly, my breasts and even on my face and in my hair. I didn't know what she was doing at the time but later I would come to recognise it. She was marking me with her scent. I reeked of her. It was her way of taking possession of me.

This task completed to her satisfaction, she suddenly jumped to her feet. She seemed mighty pleased with herself for she was chuckling in an odd way and she began to dash about the beach jumping up on rocks and giving vent to long bursts of her unfathomable tongue. Finally she dashed to a low cliff bordering the cove, clambered up and, with a grace that would have made an Olympic diver despair, launched herself off into the sea. She vanished underwater for a long time and then emerged by the side of a rock protruding out of the sea perhaps a hundred yards off the beach. She clambered up this rock, perched herself on top and began to sing.

It was the first time I ever heard her sing and, to this day, I can close my eyes and still hear the haunting ululating melodies of that eerie yet compelling refrain that drifted across the water to me as I squatted there on the beach in my misery. Forgive me but I find no words adequate enough to describe that song. Perhaps had I been a poet or a musician I might have found some way to express that mesmerising melody in words. It was enchanting in the fullest meaning of that word; as if it cast a spell over you, hypnotising you and touching you in deep forgotten places in your soul you never even knew existed. Oh God how I wish I could have recorded it. How I wish I could reproduce it. As it was, even in the desolated despair of my violation, I sat there entranced and wished it would never end.

She sang for I suppose about twenty minutes which was short by her standards. I have heard her sing for hours on end. But she ended her song and plunged back into the water to return to the beach. Perhaps she thought she was neglecting me. I huddled abjectly as she strode up to me and talked to me. Of course I had no idea what she was saying but she made her point clear as she grasped my hair and pulled me to me feet. She made as if to lead me away by dragging me by my hair put I squealed and patted her hand with mine. She stopped with a strange frown and growled at me. This I was to learn indicated that she was mildly annoyed with me. If she hissed at me and bared her teeth then she was really pissed with me. I shook my head furiously and pointed at her hand in my hair. Her puzzlement grew. Shaking the head meant something different in her body language. She had other ways to express emphatic negatives with gestures. But I held my ground stubbornly, patted her hand once more and held out my own to her.

Slowly she grasped the point and relinquished her grip in my hair, taking hold of my wrist instead to lead me. It was a minor victory but a landmark in our relationship for it was the first time we ever managed any inter-communication between us even though all I had managed to convey was that I didn't like to be pulled around by my hair and, if she must drag me around, then take my arm instead. It was a major concession to win. Thereafter she would pull me along by my arm. She would only grab my hair if she was angry with me.

She led me along the beach and round the rocks along the shore line. We had to wade through some shallow water full of seaweed. You'll think me foolish but I remember being afraid that a crab might nip my toes. In the next little bay I had a surprise for there was an old derelict, rusting fishing boat stranded on the rocks there. It was full of holes and would obviously never float again even if she had not, as I was to learn, already stripped it of anything of use to her.

She unceremoniously dumped me on the sand and strode over to this boat. Hanging off the side of this boat into the water was a length of nylon rope and, as she hauled it up, I saw that it was attached to a largish sac fashioned it seemed out of some old fishing net. She had, I was to learn, a genius for scavenging the detritus of human society for her own purposes. At the time though I was puzzled for I had started to think that she was primitive, even bestial in a way. I was clearly not thinking properly. The belt around her waist and the ornamentation she wore were clear signs that she was possessed of creative tool manipulating intelligence. The contents of the bag puzzled me further. It seemed to be full of odd knobbly, barnacle encrusted pieces of dark grey rock. As she carried the bag back toward me however I took a closer look. They were oysters. I did not know it at the time but there were significant beds of oysters around the island and she guarded them jealously and harvested them diligently.

She squatted down on the sand beside me and emptied the shellfish onto the ground. Then she took, from her belt, a short but sturdy knife set in a handle of what appeared to be bone. I blinked in surprise for it was the first irrefutable indication that she used tools and it appeared to be steel as well; fashioned perhaps from some odd piece of metal. She used this knife to pry open the oysters. I would later see that some shellfish she could crack open in her teeth but the tough gnarled oysters defeated even her formidable dentures. She extracted the meat from the inside of the oysters and began to feed it to me. By this I mean she literally fed me with her fingers as if I was a baby incapable of feeding myself.

I hadn't eaten for I suppose nearly twenty four hours but even so I had never eaten oysters. They didn't exactly figure too much on the menu back in Iowa. So I was a little reluctant to eat them to begin with. But she was persistent and eventually I tried them. To my surprise I quite enjoyed them. An expert later told me that this type of oyster, although edible, was not considered one of the gourmet types you'd find in high class restaurants. They were almost certainly a species called, in the Latin, *Pinctada radiate* which were harvested for other reasons than their edible qualities. Those other purposes would have become clear had I known that the common name for the species was Gulf Pearl Oyster, one of the most widely distributed species of pearl producing oysters whose range extended from the Mediterranean Sea to the shores of Australia and Japan.

We were in luck too for, as she conscientiously fed me, she opened one oyster to find a small pearl resting inside. She crooned in delight and dashed to the boat to return with a small tin. It appeared to be an old tobacco tin but inside she kept her treasure. It was half full of pearls. Reverently the new find was placed inside and the box resealed and replaced in its hiding place. I know little about the value of pearls but there must have been a considerable amount's worth in that tin.

Once I had been fed, she led me by the wrist once more into the interior of the island near the old ruined villa. Here she led me to the strangest feature of the island yet. In a hollow beneath some rocks was a pool of clear cool fresh water. How that pool of water came to be there on that otherwise parched island I do not know. Perhaps it bubbled up from some subterranean aquifer of perhaps gathered in that hollow from precipitation gathered on the surrounding rocks. Yet it must have been regularly replenished otherwise it would have quickly evaporated under the hot Aegean sunshine. Whatever the mysterious source of it was, it was a Godsend for it was the only source of freshwater on the island other than the occasional rainfall. I could drink my fill.

Once I had quenched my thirst she pulled me into the shade of the little olive grove and there she used me again. It seemed throughout that day she was on a mission to violate me in as many different places around the island as she could. She took me on the crest of the knoll I had first fled to. Then a little later she pulled me to the beach where I had first landed on the island and had me there as well. That was somewhat different for that time she took me laid flat on my back with my legs over her shoulders as she pounded her organ into me. She withdrew as she climaxed as well and drenched me with her semen from my face to my loins, marking me with her strong scent even more unmistakeably. Under this assault I observed another curiosity about her. She not only ejaculated from her penis as she came to orgasm but also from her vagina as well. The clear liquid from her vagina gushed out in a stream down her thighs. She must have needed a high liquid intake for she seemed to expend gallons of it over me.

In all I suppose she used me about six times that first day which was quite restrained by her standards. I have known her to pleasure herself on me up to over a

63

dozen times in a single day. Perhaps that long swim, dragging me, had sapped her strength. Although I found it easier to take after that first assault, by the end of that day I was exhausted, worn out and abused; my body covered in bruises where she had gripped me in her frenzy.

She seemed to understand this for, in the evening, she pulled me to the old ruined villa where, in the shelter of some broken walls, she fashioned a bed of sorts for me from dried vegetation and some old sacking. She seemed inordinately pleased with her new toy for she petted me almost affectionately and licked my face before lying me down and curling up beside me. I lay there as the

sunset, feeling her warmth against me, and thought how I might somehow escape this monster tomorrow. Surely there must be some passing boat or ship I could hail that could rescue me. She couldn't keep me imprisoned as her plaything indefinitely. Buoyed by these optimistic thoughts I drifted into slumber. I would have felt less confident had I known that I was destined to remain on that island for the better part of the next six months.

Chapter Four

When I awoke the next morning I was alone. I rose up from my bed amidst the ruins of the villa and peered around cautiously. There was no sign of her. Carefully I tip-toed out from the ruins and conducted a quick scan of the surroundings. The little olive grove was quite deserted other than the small creatures with which I shared the island. These seemed busy at this early hour. There was a little dark grey bird singing from the scrub at the edge of the olive grove. It had a musical voice I found quite soothing. I was to become familiar with that little bird and the mate he found to build his nest with over the coming weeks. He became a friend of mine and I would wake each morning to his singing. An ornithologist friend of mine told me, from my description, that it was probably a Sardinian Warbler, a common species throughout the Mediterranean.

There were butterflies on the wing as well as other insects and, hunting them presumably, was a gecko clinging to the side of a half collapsed wall of the villa. These, geckos, by the way had an eerie, mournful mewing cry you often heard at night, which frightened me until I discovered that the source of the cry was just a harmless little lizard. There were other lizards too; tiny little, quicksilver wall lizards that skittered around in the rubble of the villa and the dry stone walls that surrounded the olive grove. Much later I was able to put a name to these wall lizards but I shall withhold that identification here. Apparently different species of wall lizards have very marked distribution patterns within the Aegean Islands and an expert herpetologist (which is someone who studies amphibians and reptiles) would be able to locate my island within a geographical range on the basis of my identification of those lizards.

One life form was conspicuously absent however.

Of my saviour and tormentor of the day before there was not a sign to be seen. With great caution I began to explore the rest of the island looking for her. After scouring all over for her for the next hour I finally came to the conclusion that she was nowhere on the island. I was completely alone.

I climbed to the top of the rocky knoll, which was the highest point on the island, to take stock of my situation. As I did so I came upon a remarkable bird perched on the side of a small cliff. It was a beautiful slender falcon, dark grey on the mantle and wings but a lovely russet red chest and belly and a strikingly marked face of white with a black mask. It really was a most handsome creature and, as it took to the air in alarm at my approach, it was incredibly sleek in flight with long pointed wings. A pair of these falcons nested on that cliff and, once again, my ornithologist friend was able to identify them from my description. They have a fittingly beautiful name to go by since they are named after Eleanor of Arborea, a 14th century warrior regent and a legendary heroine of Sardinia. Apparently Eleanora's Falcons breed on Mediterranean islands in the spring to take advantage of the vast hordes of swallows and swifts that migrate through the region at that time of year since they are one of the few birds of prey fast and agile enough to catch these birds in flight. I'm told that around two thirds of the world's entire population of these falcons breed around the Greek islands. There are possibly only about six and a half thousand of them left in the world. Let us hope that they hold out long in these last refuges.

I perched on a rock at the top of the knoll and considered my situation glumly. Now that I had the leisure to look at it properly, the view from the knoll offered few grounds for optimism. The Aegean Sea is pretty crowded with islands but I seemed to have fetched up on one of the more remote ones. Apart from some islets, just promontories of bare rock really, close by, the only other discernible land visible was a tiny sliver right out on the horizon. It was so distant in fact that it was invisible from down at sea level and you could only see it from the elevated location atop the knoll. It might as well have been on Mars for all the chance I had of reaching it and there were not the slightest grounds for assuming it was inhabited in any case.

Doubtless had I been the heroine in an 18th century castaway romance I would have already been planning to build a boat from bits of driftwood and olive trees. But I was a hippy girl from Iowa not Robinson Crusoe and I wouldn't have had a clue how to start. What would I have even used as tools? The only tool I had seen so far had been on the belt of that person now conspicuous by her absence.

By this time I was beginning to be in two minds about the disappearance of my companion of the day before. On the one side I was sort of relieved that she'd apparently had her wicked way with me and then upped and gone, which made her not a lot different from a bunch of guys I'd known. She had, after all, abused me pretty badly and I was still scared to Hell of her. I could even still smell her scent on me and I shuddered at the thought of her rapacious sexual appetite. On the other hand however, even on short acquaintance, it was obvious that she was a sight more capable of surviving on this island than I was. She might have saved me from the sea but if she'd now just abandoned me then the prognosis for my survival for any length of time looked fairly gloomy.

This was an inescapable conclusion brought sharply into focus by the hollow rumbling in my belly. I was hungry... damn hungry and I had not the faintest idea as to how I was going to feed myself. All I'd eaten the day before were a few oysters which didn't exactly amount to a healthy balanced diet. There was, as far as I could see, damn all in the way of food on this island. Doubtless there were shellfish and crabs around the rocks and in the pools but I'd no idea which sorts were edible even if I figured out a way of opening them or, in the case of crabs, making them palatable. I could hardly live on a diet of wall lizards either. For one thing they were too small and in any case the thought of raw lizard wasn't too appetising even if I could manage to catch them. I didn't know if any of the bushes had berries on them that could be eaten and the olive trees were of no use. Olives don't bear fruit until the fall and it was springtime now. I was going to get hungrier yet.

Unable to either escape or survive on my own my attention focussed on the possibilities of rescue and this was the one area in which I thought I ought to be doing something active. The clear blue sea around me was devoid of any sign of human activity for the moment but surely, in a sea so heavily used by shipping as the Aegean, some boat had to happen along sooner or later. Also, by now, my disappearance should have been reported, hopefully, and there would be people looking for me. I had this rosy image of air sea rescue boats and helicopters scouring the sea for me.

Fat chance! I discovered much later that the discovery and subsequent investigation of my disappearance had reached levels of bungling incompetence that were farcical even by the spectacularly high standards set by Greek officialdom. It turns out that nobody had even noticed my disappearance from the ship and never would have until some steward or other discovered my belongings and passport after the ship had docked and most of the passengers had disembarked at its destination. He handed my things into the purser who seemed to regard the affair as more a case of lost property than anything else, as if I'd just gone up and left the ship, abandoning all my possessions and passport in a fit of absentmindedness. The purser had dutifully handed in my possessions to the port authorities which in this case consisted of some fat and somnolent man in a run-down quayside office who promptly sat on them for the next three days waiting for somebody to claim them. In the meantime the ship's captain, in an uncharacteristic concern for his timetable, had turned the ship around and sailed away. After nobody came to claim my possessions it slowly occurred to the dockside official that he ought to raise himself from his customary stupor and hand them in to the local police.

Police forces in the Aegean islands are not noted for their penetrating intuition and investigatory zeal. The duty sergeant at the police station followed the same erroneous deduction that I'd inexplicably left the ship without my possessions and conducted a few days of desultory inquiries among the local population to determine if anybody had come upon this American girl anywhere. Well it wasn't the biggest island in the Aegean and it seems incredible in hindsight that it took the police nearly four days to finally conclude that I was nowhere on the place. Only then, given that I had clearly boarded the ship at its starting point and equally as clearly not disembarked at its destination, did it occur to anyone that I must have vanished somewhere en route. But when and where?

Faced at last with a serious missing person inquiry, the police now rounded up all the passengers that had disembarked from the ship and interrogated them with a view to determining when exactly I had last been seen. Well if you wanted to amass a dossier of confusing and conflicting reports then you'd do worse than call upon a collection of excitable, eager to please Greeks to provide it. By the time this baffling body of testimony had been examined it was clear that nobody had the faintest idea when or where I'd vanished from the ship.

Compounding the problem was the fact that the

very course of the ship was somewhat vague. Some of the shipping in the Aegean was wont to follow what might be charitably described as haphazard routing. There was nothing for it but to run the ship in question down somewhere on the far side of the Aegean and interview the crew. This naturally took more time and even then was not conclusive. Even the ship's captain could not retrace his course with any certainty. Somebody later suggested that the captain might in fact have been somewhat reluctant to furnish exact details about his course. Smuggling was rife in the Aegean and many ship's masters were not above availing themselves of this welcome supplement to their income.

By this time, of course, it was vanishingly unlikely that I could be still alive at all and when a search mission was finally mounted it was done in a rather half-hearted sort of way and in completely the wrong place before the authorities sadly called it off and forwarded my possessions, via the American embassy, to my parents regrettably informing them that I was missing, presumed drowned. Mom and Pa, bless them, refused to believe it and flew straight out to Greece where they spent weeks thumping on desks demanding that the authorities conduct a proper and though search for their missing daughter. Spurred on by my indignant parents and the goading of the American embassy the search was resumed but again in the wrong area and with predictably futile results. My Pa even hired a motor launch and spent some time searching the islands himself. In the end though even my parents bowed to the inevitable and returned home to Iowa to grieve and conduct a ceremony of remembrance in our church.

Not many people ever get to read their own obituary but I did. I also got the gist of the parson's sermon at my remembrance ceremony. at our branch of the Episcopalian Church of Iowa, from my sister. He described me as a lost soul of Christ wandering the world in search of meaning. He prayed that in the end I had found what I was looking for and was now come to grace and sat at the side of my Lord in heaven. He might have felt less confident about the well-being of my immortal soul had he known that I was alive and well and currently being fucked up to a dozen times a day by a sexually besotted siren.

But all this knowledge lay in the future and, as I sat on the knoll, gloomily contemplating my options, the thought that there was an active hunt out for me sustained my morale. All I had to do, it seemed, was to find some way of indicating my presence on the island. Now, in every castaway story I had ever read, the hero always lights a fire to alert passing ships of his whereabouts. The recommended strategy was to put green wood or vegetation onto the fire to raise a good column of visible smoke. So light a fire... simple huh?

Great! How? I'd done enough camping around at festivals and so on to know that you can start a fire by rubbing two sticks together as long as one of them happens to be a match. Other than that I hadn't a clue about how to achieve combustion. I guess I wasn't cut out for this survivalist stuff. So I had to think of something else.

I noticed the contrails of a jet airliner high overhead and that got me thinking in another direction. The other thing that stranded castaways always did was spell out a message in rocks on the beach of their desert island. Well surely I could manage that. With renewed purpose I set off for the little beach I had first landed on the island on. I spent the next hour or so collecting rocks and laying them out in a pattern I fondly imagined would spell out the word HELP from the air. I had nearly finished this labour when it suddenly occurred to me, for some reason, that a Greek pilot might not be able to understand the English word "help". Thus I spent an extra half an hour or so rearranging the rocks to spell out the international call sign SOS instead.

When I stood back to observe the result I had to admit that it wasn't very convincing. The beach was so tiny and space so limited that a helicopter pilot would just about have to be hovering about a hundred feet overhead to make head or tail out of my message. I climbed back up the knoll to observe it from the vantage point of elevation and it looked like a fairly random collection of rocks to be frank. It was hardly an unmistakeable distress signal.

One thing I did do on that beach was recover my sari that her ladyship had torn off me and so negligently tossed aside the previous day before making her intentions upon my exposed body so abundantly clear. Although it was good to have some sort of covering again, my dismal attempts at a distress signal made me realise that I was going to have to sacrifice it once more because the next thing that occurred to me, you see, was to raise some sort of flag. Well the only piece of material that would suit that purpose on the entire island was my sari. Having said that, my sari would be eminently suitable. It was a light but highly colourful square of fabric that should be easily visible.

With renewed purpose I set out to find a flagpole.

Here the plan came unstuck. Scour that island as I might, the longest piece of wood I could find was an old, twisted tree branch washed up on the shoreline about six feet long. Perhaps some of the branches on the olive trees might have been longer had someone thoughtfully provided an axe or, better still, a chainsaw for obtaining them. Still I had to use what I had. I lugged that branch up on to the top of the knoll and, resigning myself to nudity once more, tied the corners of my sari onto the branch before jamming the end into a crevice in the rocks and raising my flag. It was hardly the most dramatic flag raising since the marines on Iwo Jima and, when I stood back to take a look, the results were sadly disappointing. A helpful feature of putting up a flag is a breeze for it to fly in. There wasn't a breath of wind and my sari hung limply to the ground like a piece of garbage caught on a twig. You could just about discern that it was a human artifice if you squinted at it carefully from no more than about ten feet away.

I scratched my head despondently. Being a castaway on a deserted island was proving to be more difficult than I had thought. Then it occurred to me that if I could find another piece of wood of a similar length I could stretch my sari between them and at least increase its visibility. It wasn't a brilliantly innovative idea but it was the best I could do and, in any case, better than doing nothing at all. Wearily I started back down toward the beach. I was just wending my way through the scrub close to the beach when I saw her emerge from the sea and begin to wade ashore.

Chapter Five

Hastily I cowered down and hid behind a bush, regarding her fearfully. She shook her head and spat a gush of water from her mouth. I saw the flaps on her shoulder blades flex and a stream of water expelled from beneath them. I think she did this to rid her throat and gills of water before opening the respiratory tract to her lungs. She took a deep breath and strode purposefully ashore. She had been busy it seemed and her morning's toil looked somewhat more fruitful than mine had been. In one hand she carried a short harpoon with a wicked looking barbed point to it. It had evidently been used to some effect for in the same hand she carried four largish fish on length of cord passed through their gills. In her other hand she had one of the sacks she fashioned from old fishing nets. In it were two sizeable lobsters still alive. She'd been out shopping it seemed. Breakfast had arrived.

She seemed to notice the sign I'd laid out on the beach. She looked at it for a few seconds as I held my breath and then gave a little snort, which was the closest she came to a shrug, and walked on ignoring it. She probably thought I'd just been amusing myself playing with stones. She never seemed to attach any significance to it and never removed it. It's probably still there to this day. She paused again and sniffed the air before letting out a loud ululating cry. Instinctively I knew that that cry was directed at me. In fact, from then on, that was the cry she invariably used to summon me when I was any distance away or when she was newly returned to the island. I never quite decided whether it was simply a call of command or whether it was her name for me or maybe a little of both. Whatever it was I quickly learned to recognise it and nearly as quickly learned to obey the summons.

I obeyed it now. I'd learned yesterday that there was no place to run or hide from her on this tiny island and any attempt to do so would be futile. In any case there were other imperatives demanding my obedience. I was starving and the burdens in her hand were food. Nervously then I stepped out from behind the bushes and out onto the beach to stand in front of her, shuffling my feet for all the world like a naughty schoolgirl summonsed before the head teacher for some misdemeancur.

She gave a little purr of satisfaction but then stared more closely at me and voiced what I can only describe as a short growl of exasperation. I suppose I didn't look a pretty sight. My morning's labours had left me dirty and dishevelled. She dropped her burdens on a flat rock and stalked up to me. She sniffed at me carefully and suspiciously. I suppose she may have thought that somebody might have been around taking advantage of her absence to violate her property while she was out at the shops. Seemingly satisfied that I had nobody's scent on me but her own, she then picked me up and, turning on her heel, strode down to the water's edge. I do mean she picked me up as well. She just grabbed me without warning, tucked me under one arm and walked straight into the sea with me squirming and protesting loudly in her grip. "Hey! What are you doing? Put me down damn you!"

She ignored my feeble remonstrance and waded up to her waist upon which she unceremoniously dumped me into the sea. I came spluttering to the surface still protesting and she grabbed a hold of me and began to wash me. I swear I'm not making this up. She held me in one hand and scrubbed me with her free hand, removing all the dirt I'd accumulated during my morning's travails. If this indignity alone was not enough, after she'd cleaned my body to her satisfaction, she then dunked my head under the water three or four times, wringing out my hair and wiping the dirt from my face. Once she was satisfied that I was fit to be seen in her company she carried me back to the shore and planted me firmly on a flat ledge of rock, growled at me and made a flat downward motion with her the palm of her hand. I got the gist. "Stay where you are!" She'd put me out to dry.

I sat on the rock watching her sullenly as she squatted down on another rock and attended to her own grooming. She had a sort of comb that looked as if it was fashioned out of a fish bone or something and she used it to tease out the tangles in her long silver hair. Once she had completed this task she walked over to me and subjected my hair to the same treatment. My hair hadn't seen a brush in three days and it was a tangled mess but she persevered at it although none too gently at times as she worked the knots out of it. My temper was not improved by this tugging at my locks and I cussed her in no uncertain terms although I knew she couldn't understand a word. Finally she had my hair into some semblance of order and she stroked it, purring to herself contentedly.

She might have been contented but I certainly wasn't. The assaults on my dignity had left me in a deeply rebellious mood and I was sulking pretty badly by then. To my horror she then decided that my appearance required just one last little touch to make it perfect. She gave that low little growling sound in the back of her throat that was becoming all too familiar and her penis quivered into life, growing enormously erect even as I watched. It was the last straw. I backed away shaking my head firmly. "No way! Out of the fucking question!" I told her decisively.

I might as well have been quoting Shakespeare or reeling off the chemical formula for formaldehyde for all the good it did. She gave me a commanding growl that I was coming to recognise as the command to assume a position for her to pleasure herself on me. I clamped my legs shut rigidly and glared at her. "I said no! Go away! Leave me alone!" Seeing that I was being uncooperative she grabbed hold cf me. I then did something damn foolish. I was so resentful by this time I flung my hand out and slapped her face.

I knew immediately that it was a very bad idea. Her eyes were like poisonous green daggers as she stared at me and she drew back her lips from her terrifying teeth and hissed at me. I cowered back, deeply alarmed and well aware that I was really in trouble now. She pushed me aside and jumped up to walk back down the beach to the water's edge. For a second I thought she was just walking away in disgust but she stopped by the water and rummaged about in the flotsam along what you'd call the tide line had the Aegean had any tides worth talking about. As I watched her fearfully she picked something up, hefted it in her hands and turned back to walk towards me purposefully. When I saw what she was carrying in her hand I jumped to my feet in alarm. It was a short piece of old planking washed up on the beach, maybe a foot long, four inches wide and perhaps a half an inch thick. I didn't know what she intended to do with it but I was pretty certain it wasn't something I was going to enjoy. I turned and bolted.

I don't suppose I got twenty feet before she caught me, grabbing me by my hair and dragging me back to the rock ledge. I was squealing in pain and fear and pleading piteously. "I'm sorry! I'm sorry. Please don't hurt me! I'm sorry." My pathetic entreaties were like the seed that fell on barren ground. She planted herself on the rock ledge and hauled me over her knee face down. I squirmed furiously but she took a firm grip, lifted that plank above my wriggling backside and proceeded to spank me. I think I've mentioned her uncanny strength before. Well writhing about over her knee and squealing my head off as that plank fell time and time again across my burning buttocks I could testify feelingly to that strength. With a firm hand she did a thorough job on my stinging backside and the backs of my thighs.

I struggled mightily but to no avail in her grip. This was a woman, after all, that I know for a fact could catch moray eels in her bare hands. A little wriggling hippy girl wasn't going to slow her down for an instance. Had I had any thoughts other than the blazing agony in my rear portions, I might have reflected that my previous attempts to advertise my presence on the island to passing shipping were put to shame because, had there been any ship within five miles, they must have surely heard my howling as she paddled my rump for me. Finally she pushed me off her knee and I dropped to the sand clutching my backside and blubbering pathetically. She growled at me and treated me to a diatribe in her baffling tongue whilst waving that plank under my nose. I didn't understand the words but the meaning was clear enough. "Behave yourself or expect more of the same."

She dropped to her knees on the sand in front of me and grunted at me meaningfully as she grasped her erection in her hand. Wisely this time I didn't argue but turned resignedly on my knees, parted my legs and presented myself for her. She grasped my hips and impaled me, pounding me like a piston, her hips slapping away painfully at my smarting rear. I gritted my teeth, snivelled feebly and endured it. It was one of the occasions when she didn't allow herself to come inside me but withdrew at the moment of her ejaculation and spurted that enormous flood of semen all over me. She then meticulously smeared it all over the parts of my body she had missed, to mark me thoroughly with her scent, and, just to prove a point it seemed to me, she forced my mouth open and made me lick her fingers clean.

Finally she sniffed at me critically and, satisfied, released me and I hunched up on the sand in abject humiliation and glowered at her. "Well I hope I smell nice enough for you now." I told her bitterly. My sarcasm was wasted. She just sat back on her haunches purring softly and looking mighty pleased with herself. Finally she rose with a little wheeze that might have been a sigh as if she was thinking, "Well that's enough fun and games for the moment. Back to work." She walked over and recovered the efforts of her morning's fishing and came back to me holding out her hand.

"Now what?" I demanded fractiously. She growled at me and so I hastily put my hand out. "All right! All right! I'm coming damn you!" She gripped me by the wrist and I allowed myself to be led away sulkily but obediently. She took me back to the olive grove and sat me down on the ruins of the stone wall. She disappeared for a couple of minutes before reappearing carrying an old rusted tin box she must have had concealed somewhere. She had caches of these treasures of hers hidden all over the island I discovered later. From this she pulled a wicked looking curved knife. With this knife she started to clean the fish she'd caught.

Even in my seditious mood I started to take an interest in proceedings. I was very hungry and it seemed as if at least there might be something to eat in the offing. The fish looked quite substantial and my stomach was beginning to nibble at the back of my throat. I think the fish were some kind of sea bream. I'm no ichthyologist but a marine biologist, I described them to later, said he thought they were most probably Common Dentex or possibly the closely related Pink Dentex. I do know that they must have been common in the sea around the island for they often figured on our menu. The lobsters in the bag were, I think, Spiny Lobsters; a common species in the Mediterranean and fished for commercially.

My hopes of lunch took a severe blow however. As she cleaned the fish she removed the innards and popped them into her mouth and chewed them in evident satisfaction. This bit was pretty disgusting actually. She even lopped the heads off the fish and crunched them between her teeth with something approaching relish. I stared at her in horror. Surely she didn't expect me to do the same! She did however fillet the fish and lay the fillets out along a stone. I was still horrified however. I couldn't possibly eat raw fish. I knew that some cultures ate raw fish but small town Iowa wasn't one of them. This was in '72 remember, before sushi bars sprang up all over the place.

She didn't make any attempt to offer me the fish however. Instead she started to gather stones and arranged them in a circle. Within this circle she piled some dried grass and twigs and overlaid them with pieces of scrub wood, dead branches and old driftwood (I noticed bitterly incidentally that the plank of wood she'd spanked me with was conspicuously absent from the materials. Presumably she had other purposes for that.) In astonishment I realised she was building a fire. Remembering my earlier confusion regarding the mysteries of attaining combustion I leaned forward to watch carefully how she was going to light it. By this time I wouldn't have been surprised if she'd pulled a Zippo out of her box of tricks. She didn't do that but what she did do was almost as astonishing. She extracted a tiny little magnifying lens and with this focussed the beams of the sun into a bright spot on the dried grass. The spot glowed red hot and began to smoulder. She bent forward to blow on it gently and, in no time at all, she had a fire burning. It took her literally seconds. I was outclassed in the backwoods frontier man category.

She skewered the fillets on lengths of green wood and grilled them carefully in the flames. I could smell the fish cooking and my stomach jumped in renewed hope. My earlier resentment was forgotten and soon as was crouching by the fire beside her, eagerly watching the fish brown in the flames. She purred deeply and reached a hand out to pet me affectionately. Then blowing on the fillets to cool them she began to feed me the fish with her fingers. I don't know exactly what those fish were but I can tell you they were absolutely delicious. They weren't seasoned bar the flavour of the wood smoke and they were perhaps a little charred on the outsides in places but I was so hungry they tasted like ambrosia. The flesh was firm and white and just heavenly. I wasn't much of a fish eater. I wasn't much of any kind of flesh eater in fact despite my origins in a red meat county in Iowa. During my hippy wanderings I'd been a brown rice and noodles kind of girl. That fell by the wayside. My mistress and provider was essentially a predator. Vegetarianism wasn't an option. I wolfed that fish down. I didn't let her feed me completely. I greedily plucked off pieces myself as well to eat. She seemed to think it was very clever of me... like a puppy learning a new trick.

After she'd fed me, I drank water from the pool and laid back against the old stone wall in the sunshine; feeling replete and content for the first time since my arrival on the island while she meticulously cleared away all the detritus of my meal. I was feeling kind of sleepy but even so I retained enough sense to realise that what I had just witnessed was incredible. It was easy to think of this woman who walked (and swam) the length of her days completely naked was somehow primitive and backwards. Yet she had just displayed a level of sophistication and know-how that was quite simply breath-taking. It wasn't just her easy familiarity with fire although that in itself was remarkable enough.

I was already, you see, slowly coming to the conclusion that this woman was not human. No, that's not right. She was human right enough... she was just a different species of human. She was not Homo sapiens. Call her for the sake of argument Homo aquaticus although I'm sure any taxonomist would howl in derision at that choice of Latin name. She was a hominid, closely related to us if you like but no more than, say, the extinct species of Home erectus or Home neanderthalensis that we know from the fossil record. She was a completely separate species of human being from me; a semi aquatic or amphibious human evolved for a life in and around the ocean edges. I'll discuss this later in this story but suffice it to say for the moment that, if this was true then it raised a number of very interesting questions.

Take her use of fire. Why would a species that lived a semi-aquatic life in warm oceans ever need to develop the technology of fire? She didn't need it to cook her prey for instance. She didn't eat any of that cooked fish. She gave it all to me. For her part she was quite happy to consume her fish raw. A species evolved for life in the sea didn't need fire for warmth or protection either.

Yet she not only was familiar with fire but also used a very sophisticated, advanced technology to produce it. Using a lens to produce fire was a hell of a lot more technologically advanced than rubbing two boy scouts together. Even primitive Homo sapiens never picked that trick up. Perhaps significantly the earliest records we have of the use of burning lenses come from the writings of Ancient Greece. Aristophanes for instance mentions it in his play "The Clouds". The Olympic torches of ancient Greece were supposed to be ignited directly by the Gods, unsullied by human hands and so were lit with burning lenses. So did this woman or her kind pick up the idea from contact with Homo sapiens? It was hard to believe that she could make her own glass or grind lenses.

Yet the most incredible thing of all was not that she could make fire in such a sophisticated way or even that she could use it to cook food that she didn't need to cook. The astonishing thing was that she knew that I had to have my food cooked. That bespoke of a level of intelligence and understanding that was frankly amazing. How could she have known so much about my kind to know that certain foods I could not eat without their first being treated with fire? It shows a level of knowledge far beyond what anybody might know of her kind. Perhaps though she didn't.

I have one theory which might or might not hold water. I found out later that there were indeed foods which she would cook and eat. Certain tough meats for instance she would roast before devouring which proved to my satisfaction that she occasionally preyed on the land as well as in the sea. It still beggars the question of why she should feed cooked fish to me. My theory is that perhaps the very young of her species needed their food tenderised in such a way before they could eat it in much the same way as very young children of our species need to have their food specially prepared to make it possible to eat. In defence of this theory it has to be noted that she seemed to treat me like a small child, washing me, feeding me by hand and so forth.

This may sound crazy. Surely you would think that she must have realised that I was an adult. Yet much of her behaviour towards me was that of parent towards a child. Is that how she really saw me? Perhaps the closest parallel is the relationship between a person and a dog. We don't treat our pet dogs as equal partners after all do we? We treat them in much the same way we'd treat a precocious child. Petting them when they're good, smacking them when they do something we disapprove of and generally not trusting them to do anything without our supervision. animal psychologists have long noted that, as a result, dogs retain juvenile behavioural traits throughout their lives and never attain the mature characteristics that wolves, for example, will come to in the wild. I think she treated me as a pet; or at least as a pet sometimes, a plaything at others, a child occasionally and never as an equal.

One of the few people I have ever trusted with this story had another theory that related to this. He suggested that she was herself juvenile by the standards of her species; perhaps an unmated individual that was literally using me as practice; a sort of surrogate for the children she had never had in the same way that young girls of our species play with dolls or play at being mothers. He also raised the uncomfortable question that it might have been pathological behaviour; the desperate yearnings of an unmated person who, as a result of the dramatic decline of her own species, had little chance of mating, and therefore no offspring, who had captured a human being and used them as a substitute for children she could never have; an irrational last attempt at survival of a dying species. That is a thought that has haunted me for years.

There is much in this theory but I still always felt that it didn't answer all the questions. It is true that it is impossible to judge the behaviour of an entire species on the actions of a single individual. She might have indeed been insane. But somehow I don't think so. She exhibited too many examples of rational and complex behaviour that demonstrated high intelligence, creative thinking and purposeful logic. She was frighteningly capable in so many ways. If anything I was the one who felt inadequate and incapable beside her. She may not have had the benefit of a Cambridge Doctorate to her name but I have the feeling that she was far more brilliant than me. Perhaps in hindsight I was just a little lost child compared with her. I think also we should be wary of attributing behaviour and morality to an entirely different species for which such things are meaningless. God knows we have a hard enough time understanding the motives and thought processes of different cultures within our own species let alone those of a completely different, intelligent creature.

The one thing that may seem baffling is her continual use of me as a sexual plaything. It would seem to contradict the theory that she viewed me as a child. After all the sexual abuse of children is not morally acceptable behaviour for Homo sapiens but then again I may be attempting to impose the morality of my species upon her.

Then again I think she did indeed view me in adult terms when she used me for her pleasure. I think in fact that she may have even thought that she had the moral right to do so. Certainly her other actions to me were, within the context of the situation, extremely moral by any standards. She did after all save my life. Further than that, throughout that summer, she went to extraordinary lengths to keep me well and protected. I think there was more than just her desire to keep her toy girl healthy for her own base purposes in that. I believe she had a genuine compassion and affection for me which she showed in a myriad of ways and not least in the manner of our parting. She might have considered that the sexual pleasure she derived from me was but due payment for what I owed her. She may have been right. Because of her, I have lived a good and fulfilled life. I think sacrificing a paltry six months of that life to be the sex toy of a fascinating and mysterious creature was a small price to pay for that gift... don't you?

I think that may come close to the truth. She saved my life. I think that, by her own moral standards, meant that she owned me. I was her possession. I might have been her dearest possession and one for whom she had the greatest affection but her possession nevertheless. I was her pet and I think she loved me. That didn't make us equals. I have a Red Setter called Rufus. I love him to bits but I still won't let him sit on the sofa.

Chapter Six

In many ways, the events of that day first shaped our relationship to come. I certainly learned to do more as I was told although I did still transgress on occasion. Minor misdemeanours would earn me a slap, more serious offences a spanking. That plank of wood became an essential item among our domestic appliances you might say, along with a length of insulated electric cable for when she was really pissed with me. She soon licked me into shape. Within days she had me following her around like a meek little puppy dog and if I ever wandered away she only had to call and I'd come running. I wish Rufus was as well behaved.

Oddly I settled into this relationship quite quickly. For one thing, I had no choice. I was completely dependent on her for my survival after all. I wouldn't have lasted five minutes on my own on that island and, as the days passed by, the chances of my being rescued faded away to vanishing point. There were no coast guard rescue boats and helicopters swarming about after all. I think, in the first fortnight I spent on the island, I saw one sad little smoky steamer passing on the horizon. My mistress happened to be out at sea fishing at the time and I remember jumping up and down and waving my hands frantically on top of the knoll. God knows what I thought I was going to achieve. In the infinitesimally small chance that there was somebody on the bridge of that decrepit old rust bucket who was taking their duties seriously enough to be scanning the horizon with binoculars and sighting me, God only knows what they would have thought at the sight of me hopping up and down like a demented idiot. "Damn tourists get everywhere. Why don't they put some clothes on? Have they no shame?" The steamer vanished over the horizon without the vaguest hint that anybody might have noticed me. By the way I never resorted to putting a message in a bottle. I did occasionally find bottles washed up on the shoreline but I was a bit short on writing materials.

So yes I needed her. She was keeping me alive. Having said that, I must say, that she took her responsibility for me very seriously. They call this a Chinese Obligation. In China, apparently, if you saved somebody's life then you had taken responsibility for that person away from the Gods. Therefore they were your problem now and you had to take care of them. She did this, considering the means at her disposal, very well indeed.

The sea around our island teemed with marine life and she was truly expert at harvesting it. Fish featured heavily in our diet as you would expect. Those sea bream became one of our staples but by no means the only fish we ate. There was a sort of flatfish with very widely spaced eyes that we sometimes dined on and one day she returned from her morning's fishing carrying a substantial turbot which was delicious. One bounty that we often exploited were the shoals of pilchards and mackerel that often visited the vicinity. These would frequently betray their presence by the flocks of birds wheeling overhead feeding on them or the bait fish they were chasing. I got very good at spotting these and, if she was busy doing other things, I would spend my time scouring the sea around the island for flocks of birds. If I saw one, I would rush to tell her. By this time she was more indulgent of me and I was able to take liberties with her such as take her arm to and gesture excitedly to convey the message that there was something I wanted her to see. She'd follow me and, if she thought the school of fish looked promising, she would drop what she was doing and race into the sea to catch them.

She had an interesting way of catching these more pelagic species and it might be useful to describe some of the fishing techniques she employed. For many of the rock fishes around the shores her preferred method was spear fishing or even catching fish in her bare hands. She was by no means limited to this method however. To my astonishment she was equally at home with baited hooks on lines. She had a lot of nylon mono-filament line stashed on fashioned spools around the island. I think she mostly pirated this line from the long lines used by fishermen in the Aegean. She must have been a scourge of Greek fishermen because she also used to steal their lobster pots as well and use them herself when she was too busy to go dig out lobsters from their lairs. The lines, however, she used in a number of ways.

One lazy way was to arm them with hooks baited with shellfish and lay out lines from the shore. This was one of the few fishing techniques I was actually able to help her with. I'd stand on the shore letting out the line as she swam out and placed the lines carefully along the bottom in places she knew that fish would frequent. She weighted these lines with old iron bolts or other pieces of scrap metal she salvaged from the old wrecked fishing boat. Once in place the lines caught us a surprising amount of fish; flatfish, bream, drums, gurnards, dogfish, small wrasse, mullet and jacks. We even occasionally caught small morays which was a bonus because moray eels are very tasty. The real prize however was when we managed to catch a grouper for these were the best tasting fish of all in my opinion. The deep water among the rocks at the north end of the island had a lot of grouper in it but it could be a real tussle trying to extract a good sized grouper from his hole on a hook.

Checking the baited lines was a task that eventually devolved on me and it was a task I loved. For one thing it made me actually feel useful, other than as a means of my mistress's sexual gratification, and, furthermore, it demonstrated the growing trust that she had in me in that she permitted me to perform this function. Mostly, however, I just loved the thrill of it. You never knew what you were going to catch and it was the thrill of the hunt that excited me. The bane of my life were the small fish and crabs that would rob the hooks and there were times when the line became tangled in the rocks and I'd have to solicit my mistress's assistance to swim out and free it for me. Other times some predator would get to the fish before I'd pulled the line in and you'd find the disembodied head of your catch hanging sadly on the hook. Some of these may have been sharks although we saw them rarely around the island.

It wasn't the whole story however for one day I was pulling in a small bream and close to the rocks from where I was standing a darn great Barracuda exploded from nowhere and snatched my catch straight off the line. It scared the hell out of me! Some fish I needed her help with too. I was scared to death of moray eels for example and one day, after much tugging and sweating, I managed to haul a good sized ray to the side. I thought it was a stingray and wouldn't go near it. It wasn't. It was just an ordinary Thornback Ray and she seemed quite amused by my cries for help when she came to deal with it for me. That night we feasted on ray wings.

The one fish that really gave me a scare, though, was when I came to pull the line in and there was something so strong on the end that it nearly pulled me clean off the rocks into the water. I sat on my backside and dug my heels against the rocks holding on for dear life, with the line cutting into my hands, and screamed for help. She came running, in visible agitation, and took over my burden. That fish was so strong even she had trouble pulling him in and we had the devil of a job getting it up onto the rocks. It was a rare catch so close inshore for it was a big Amberjack; so big that we couldn't eat all of it and we used the leftovers to bait our hooks with for the next two days.

For mackerel, pilchards and other surface to mid-water pelagic species however she used a different method. She'd swim out to where the shoal was with a length of line on a spool with six or more hooks baited with gull feathers and with a small weight on it. She'd literally swim into the middle of the shoal and drop this line down and jig the feathers up and down. It was deadly. The fish used to commit suicide on those feathered hooks and sometimes she'd return to shore after just a few minutes with a dozen or more fish threaded onto a length of cord hung around her shoulders. To cook them she'd prized an old piece of metal grating from the wrecked fishing boat and we propped this up on rocks over the fire to act as a griddle. They were delicious. This technique brought us bigger game too for one day she struggled ashore under the weight of a pair of big bonito she'd managed to snare.

We didn't just eat fish however. There were also shellfish and most of these I got to like especially the mussels she harvested from the rocks and the clams and oysters she fetched ashore. We ate crabs too and I developed a taste for lobster that I still have to this day. She caught squid as well and, although I would eat it, I was never that fond of it. She occasionally speared an octopus too and it was another item on our diet I had mixed feelings about. She caught prawns and crayfish which I had no problems with but I didn't much care for the sea weed she sometimes brought in. She boiled this in an old tin can she had and insisted on me eating it. She seemed to think it was good for me and she'd threaten me with the paddle if I didn't eat it all up obediently. I'd sit there chewing away sullenly for all the world like a little girl who's been told she can't have any dessert unless she eats all her broccoli.

Sea food was by no means my only source of sustenance. Occasionally we dined on birds. Seagulls I was never very fond of but just once in a while she managed to catch a duck and that was a rare treat. We'd roast it over the fire and even she would eat the cooked meat. I think she would have taken more variety of animals had they been available. I know she hunted turtles and seals for instance because she had artefacts made from their shells and skins respectively. I'm also convinced that she was perfectly capable of hunting terrestrial animals. She fashioned knife handles from bone and I found among her possessions the horns of a Mouflon; a sort of wild sheep that has been introduced to some Mediterranean islands. She was a true apex predator and feared little in the sea. She had a necklace made of sharks' teeth around her neck.

One sort of animal that definitely was not on the menu however were dolphins. We had a pod of them that used to visit the island quite often. She was always delighted to see them and she'd rush into the water to play with them; swimming around with them or holding onto their backs. They used to click and chatter with her and she used to respond in the same way. It might be fanciful but she seemed to be able to talk with them. Oh I don't mean that she could discuss the finer points of geo-politics with them or even ask after their grandmothers but there was still some sort of communication between them. There seemed to be some genuine friendship between them and, if anything, she respected them more as her equals than she did me. There was certainly no question of animosity in their relationship and she wouldn't have dreamed of hunting them I think. She rather respected them as fellow intelligent creatures with whom she shared her environment and the feeling appeared to be reciprocated.

I may be reading too much into this but I think this mutual respect and affection between the two species had deep roots. I have wondered about this a lot. We Homo sapiens kill dolphins in our fishing nets, plunder their food on industrial scales, pollute the seas and rivers they swim in, hunt them occasionally or capture them and teach them to play tricks for our entertainment in zoos. You would have thought that they'd have little time for us therefore. Yet dolphins are one of the very few wild animals on the planet that are naturally friendly to humans. Perhaps... just perhaps... that friendship has its origins in a truly non-competitive relationship... that between a semi aquatic species of hominid and a fully aquatic cetacean. Do these intelligent marine animals really see us therefore as friends because of our close relationship to this other hominid? As they say...go figure.

Whenever we had the dolphins to visit to begin with I used to sit on the shore and watch her jealously. I'd always had a bit of a thing about dolphins and I would have loved to be able to swim out and play with them. Finally though, one day she took me out, helping me swim to meet them. I felt I'd been formally introduced. It was one of the best days of my life. They let me stroke them and one even permitted me to cling onto its dorsal fin while it swam around. I'd never been happier.

But these were just interludes in what quickly settled down into a routine existence. Hunting and fishing were by no means the only tasks she had. She spent hours fashioning tools and hunting equipment for instance. I think I've mentioned that she was something of a genius in recycling the debris of human society for her own ends; any old bits of metal, tin cans, wood, bits of floating plastic, old bottles, discarded fishing nets, old corks you name it. The nest she made for me to sleep in amidst the ruins of the villa was a piece of inspired improvisation constructed out of rubble, old bits of planking, a piece of old plastic sheeting and some old sacking stuffed with grass. She would scour the shore line and the sea around for anything that might turn out to be useful.

The amount of trash that floats around in the oceans has to be seen to be believed. What an incredibly wasteful species we are. Years later I would have this impression reinforced on a journey through Africa. I saw there how the poorer people reused everything. Old tins cans and coke bottles were valuable household commodities. They never threw anything away. It made me ashamed of the profligate wastage of my own society. This girl, though, took recycling to a whole new dimension.

I've mentioned before her caches of hidden treasure. I got to see the inside of some of these and it was astonishing the sort of things she'd pick up. Some of them were a bit unsavoury. She'd pick over old carcasses for one thing because bone was a useful material which she used in all sorts of ways. Some material was plainly recovered from wrecked ships and she had bits of fabric, old brass fittings, old utensils and even some bits of crockery. Lengths of rope or twine she always salvaged as well as discarded electrical wire and, as we've seen, fishing line. She had a surprising amount of plastic in her collection since it's a material that floats readily. There was all kinds of stuff. She even had an old baseball glove that she'd found floating somewhere that she'd picked up in case it might come in useful one day. It did. I used it after my adventure with that Amberjack so that I wouldn't cut my hand on the fishing line when pulling it in, in future. Once I'd learned how from her, I used to collect mussels and shrimps from the shallow water around the island. I used an old plastic lunch box to carry them in.

As you might discern I was beginning to work to earn my keep more and more. There was not the slightest hint of compulsion about this though. Other than for sexual purposes there was no sense that she ever used me as a slave. In fact I had to work diligently to convince her that I could be of some use. I think it was almost a surprise to her to learn that I actually could be useful and relieve her of some chores. I certainly didn't mind. On the contrary I revelled in it. I think that my earlier realisation of just how useless I really was in such a survival situation had made me feel inadequate. Doing my bit for our mutual survival restored my confidence and my dignity.

This was important and in many ways I think it was the making of me. I'd been a hippy on the road for those years and I'd fancied myself to be free. My freedom had been an illusion and one propped up by my father's long suffering generosity. I'd actually lived a pampered life under the security net of the society I fancied I'd rejected for some nebulous notion of hippy freedom. Now, on that island, I learned what freedom really was. In the words of that old song "Freedom's just another word for nothing left to lose." I was naked and I had to learn to struggle with my bare hands just to stay alive and I could not have done it without her. The truth I learned is that freedom is a lonely place to be; how quickly you will abandon it in slavery to the people who will help you stay alive and how important it is that you, in turn, accept their slavery to you and take responsibility for their survival as well. These are lessons I have never forgotten. I found I could do things I never thought I could. I've never accepted anything as beyond my abilities ever since. I lost my fear on that island. You get a whole heap of time to think when you're stranded miles from anywhere.

One of the jobs for which I took responsibility was in collecting driftwood for the fire. This turned into a bit of a crisis after a couple of months. The problem was that this was one natural resource that we were using beyond its sustainability. We were burning the stuff faster than it could accumulate on the shoreline. We were being frugal with our fires; only using fire to prepare food as much as possible. Had it been winter and I'd required fire for warmth the problem would have been more acute. As it was, on cooler nights, I had to rely on her body warmth under the sacking in our nest to keep me warm. Nevertheless it was getting harder and harder to find driftwood.

We did have one resource however that we were able to call upon. One of the olive trees in the grove was dead. I don't know what killed this tree. Olive trees are nearly impossible to kill. Some of them can live to be two thousand years old. Nevertheless this tree was dead or at least apparently dead because olive trees can sometimes regenerate from their roots even when the whole top of the tree is destroyed. Reluctantly my mistress came to the conclusion that this tree would have to be sacrificed for firewood.

It turned out to be a hell of a job. Olive wood is dense and compact and even a small tree takes a hellacious amount of felling and chopping up with a crude axe. It took us three days to reduce that one tree to usable firewood. We didn't use it all for firewood of course. Olive wood is wonderful for carving and she used a good deal of it to fashion implements with, including knife handles, platters, wooden tools and a whole assortment of other things. In case you're wondering, olive wood makes a good fuel for fires. It takes a devil of an amount of time to get it burning because the wood is so dense but, once you have got it alight, it burns for a long, long time and emits a lovely aromatic smoke.

So she was busy with one thing and another on the island but she was, nevertheless, a great believer in the old adage that all work and no play makes Jill a dull girl and, topping all, among her favourite leisure activities, was me. There were few jobs she didn't feel could be made infinitely more pleasant and tolerable by taking a time out to give her pet toy girl a damn good screwing. I guess she used me about eight to ten times a day on average and often more when she was feeling particularly amorous. Most of these couplings were pretty brief affairs. We'd be doing something and she'd just give that characteristic little growl in her throat and I'd sigh, drop whatever it was I was doing and just assume the position. She'd leap aboard as it were, hammer away for a couple of minutes and leave me dripping with her copious seminal fluid, of which there seemed to be an almost endless source. Then we'd just carry on with the job in hand.

It might seem that I was badly used and, in the beginning I suppose, I felt pretty resentful of her continual abuse of me. Gradually though I just came to accept it and got on with it. It was just a part of life. I can remember once squatting on a rock, jutting out into the sea and baiting up some hooks on one of our long lines when she came up behind me with obvious intentions in mind. I just knelt forward, opened my legs and presented myself and carried on baiting my hooks while she satisfied herself and it didn't seem at all bizarre at the time. If some fisherman had sailed around the headland at that moment, God only knows what he would have made of the spectacle.

By this above do not assume that I was completely indifferent to her sexual assaults on me. Here I'm afraid I must blush with shame. It wasn't too big a step from accepting her sexual advances as an inevitable consequence of life to coming to actively enjoy it. There's an old saying that goes something along the lines of if it's going to happen anyway you might as well lie back and enjoy it. Well I wouldn't go that far but certainly her sexual predation on me became less and less unwelcome and crossed a Rubicon beyond which it actually became a source of pleasure. Even in her earliest violations of me my body had responded to her. Now as

I took a more relaxed attitude to the whole business it responded even more and I'd end up excited and often climax.

The only trouble for me was that, to begin with at least, our couplings tended to be rather short, sharp affairs. I don't know if there was a word for foreplay in her language but if there was she didn't seem to have come across it. I actually think she was quite unsophisticated when it came to sex and it reinforced the feeling I got occasionally that she was not quite mature in some ways. Given the obvious absence of her own kind I might well have been the first person with whom she had enjoyed sex. I remembered how ecstatic she'd been that first day on the beach. Maybe I'd taken her virginity damn it. Since then she hadn't been able to have enough of me but, through her lack of sexual experience, it was a pretty crude affair.

Well a quick "whim, wham, thankee ma-am" might have been all right for her but I liked to be wooed a bit more. If I'd learned anything from my dissolute days since the summer of love in '67 it was a few of the arts of the bedroom or the tent or the back of a Volkswagen bus or the back stage of rock concert or the... well you get the picture. So I might not have had much clue about survival on a barren ocean island but I did know a bit about fucking and so, in a spirit of "if you're going to do it at least do it properly" I set out to educate her in my one useful area of expertise... sex.

By this don't for a moment imagine that this placed me on an equal footing with her. She was still top dog on the island. I wasn't about to start getting above my station. Nevertheless even the most obsequious Girl Friday can learn how to manipulate her mistress after a time. She used to like to lick me and I encouraged her to do it more often because after I got used to it I used to like it. I used to especially like it if she licked my breasts and sex Of course I had no words that she could understand to tell her that I enjoyed it but I got kind of clever and I learned to imitate the purring sound she made when she was experiencing pleasure and I used it to show what I liked her to do.

Another thing I used to do was run away. I overplayed my hand on this one a couple of times and it earned me a spanking but I learned how to show her that I was just being a tease and not deliberately disobedient. She'd approach me with obvious amorous intent and I'd look at her erection and perhaps reach out and touch it coquettishly before jumping up, running away and pretending to hide. We'd play for a little while as I dodged behind rocks and bushes before letting her catch me. It always used to make her wildly excited and she'd be like a big pussy cat after I finally surrendered to her.

One thing she never learned to do was kiss properly and I don't think that kissing was part of her cultural forms of body contact. I didn't much mind this to be honest. Kissing somebody on the mouth that possesses the formidable dental equipment that she had is a bit intimidating to say the least. I did however lick her face and other parts of her to show her that she had made me happy. More problematical was using oral sex on her.

She was quite happy to lick and fondle me in those places but, to begin with, she was very wary of letting me near her sex organs with my mouth. In fact she was even cautious about letting me touch her there with my hands for the first few weeks. Slowly however she learned to trust me not to hurt her and she'd let me take her penis and stroke it. From there she'd let me stroke her female organs as well and I could often bring her to orgasm like that. It amused me that I could make her not only gush from her vagina but also ejaculate from her penis just by stroking her there.

The first time I tried to use my mouth, however, she freaked on me a bit. I'd more or less come to the point of her letting me lick her penis but when I opened my mouth and took it inside, she grabbed my hair and hissed at me. For once I wasn't intimidated though and I just looked at her submissively and imitated her purr to tell her that I wanted to do it. I opened my mouth and put my tongue out and let the tip of her penis rest on my tongue. With extreme caution and never letting go of my hair she allowed me to take her penis in my mouth and I gave her what was undoubtedly the first blow job she had ever had.

To be honest I'm not surprised that fellatio was not a common means of sexual intimacy among her kind. If you possessed a penis you wouldn't want to stick it in a mouth full of those sort of teeth either. But, once she had learned it was safe, she came to love it when I did this. It was a bit rough to do to be frank because she'd get so excited, grab my hair and pound away at my face frenziedly and nearly choke me on occasions. Also, of course, the huge quantities she ejaculated could just about drown you if you took it in the mouth. I used to have to try and time it so that I pulled away just as she came. That way I just got my face and hair drenched instead.

Another thing she came to like was being penetrated by my fingers in her vagina. I tried to encourage her more to take me in a missionary position rather than her favourite doggy style. This way I could reach behind her and wriggle my fingers inside her as she thrust away at me and it used to drive her crazy. This showed me one very interesting thing about her. I couldn't penetrate her too far without causing her discomfort. Why? Because she had at least a partially intact hymen. She might have been screwing her brains out ten times a day with her male organs but as a female she was still a virgin.

One thing I hated were the very rare times she penetrated me in the anus. She was far too big for me there and it hurt like hell. Actually I think she only used this as a sort of punishment for me; frequently after she'd given me a hard spanking. I guess she knew that it hurt and I hated it so she'd only do it to show her extreme displeasure.

Other than that I became pretty cooperative with just about anything she wanted me to do. In fact I even initiated sex between us more and more frequently; not that she needed much encouragement. Still there were times when I used sex to manipulate her mood. I remember, for instance, when she came back from fishing out among the rocks while I was gathering shellfish. She was glum and despondent. Her ears were drooping and she sat down on a rock making the odd little whining noises that she made when she was distressed. She didn't have tear ducts to the best of my knowledge. This was her way of crying. The reason for her distress was evident. In her hand she was holding the broken shaft of her favourite harpoon. Presumably she'd broken the end off on some fish and it had gone away carrying the barbed tip with it. This was a blow. Harpoons were labour intensive, highly difficult things to manufacture.

I sidled up to her and put my arms around her. I thought for a second she was going to push me away but she endured my petting. I reached out and took hold of the broken shaft and stroked it meaningfully. She grunted curiously so I transferred my hand to her penis and stroked that it the same way. It instantly sprang to attention and I purred to her softly before dropping to my knees and presenting myself for her. She gave a satisfied growl, flung the broken shaft aside and concentrated on the business to hand. Afterwards, with her morale thoroughly restored, she set about to make a new harpoon, purring to herself, and I went back to gathering shellfish, content that I'd performed my domestic duty.

In the end I could more or less get away with doing

anything with her. There were only two places I had to be careful about touching her. One place was her gills which I had to try and avoid. The other place was the ridge that ran down her spine. I could only stroke this with the utmost tenderness and care for she was incredibly sensitive there. I have a theory, which I've never been able to prove, that this ridge was actually some sort of extended sensory organ. I believe that she used it to detect vibrations and possibly subtle changes in pressure while under water; that it was in fact equivalent in function to the lateral line on a fish. As I say though I have no proof for this and it may just be a hunch.

One thing never happened throughout our sexual intercourse. I never became pregnant. I have often wondered about that. I was certainly not infertile for I had children some years later. Throughout my time on the island, I menstruated regularly and presumably ovulated too. Certainly it wasn't for lack of trying. She must have doused my womb with gallons and gallons of sperm throughout our acquaintance. Yet there was never any result to show for it. Was she then infertile? Was her hermaphrodite condition an aberration that left her infertile. I don't think it was. I have reasons to believe that hermaphroditism was normal among her kind and certainly no barrier to fertility.

So the other possibility is, that as two different species, we were simply not inter-fertile with each other; or, at least, hybridisation between our species was unlikely and rare. I suppose I should feel grateful. God knows how I would have explained it if I'd returned home after that summer with a hybrid child in my womb. Nevertheless there still remains in me just a tiny pang of regret there. If I could have hybridised with her what an extraordinary thing that would have been! What kind of person would a cross between our species have become? Imagine if you like the incredible implications that

101

would have meant for both her species and ours. It would have been a child that would quite literally have changed our view of ourselves forever. It would have changed the world. But it never happened.

Her indulgence in me was not confined to her frequent mating with me. She enjoyed me in other ways too. Even when she was working at something on the island she just liked to have me nearby and would often stop to pet me affectionately. Even after she had learned that I was quite capable of feeding and bathing myself she still would often do these things for me. She just liked doing it. She enjoyed just sitting and stroking me or tasting me with her tongue and brushing out my hair gave her immense satisfaction. She liked to plait it as well and she wound ornaments into my hair to decorate it. At such times I felt like her doll but I endured it for it gave her the most enormous satisfaction.

She liked to decorate me in other ways as well. For instance she liked to paint me sometimes. She used to make these pastes out of mud which she coloured with dyes she made from marine animals. (She used octopus ink in one of them I think) and would paint my body with curious designs and symbols. She would attend to this task most solemnly and studiously and I often had the eerie feeling that her designs had greater significance to her than mere abstract patterns.

This feeling was reinforced by an amulet she carved for me. She often made bangles or necklaces for me from bits of old fishing line hung with shells or other objects but this amulet was more important. For one thing she carved it from a piece of ivory in her possessions. For years it baffled me how she had come to own a piece of ivory. The mystery was partially solved when I showed it to an expert much later. It was, he informed me, walrus ivory, taken from the tusks of an adult walrus. That only told half the story. It blew a hole in a pet theory of mine for instance. I had at that point been coming to the opinion that her species was one of warm or tropical marine environments. Walrus, of course, live in the Arctic.

But it was not just the origin of the amulet's material that held significance. The carving itself was of highly symbolic content. It showed a clearly sexual symbolism for it had an oval loop penetrated by an obvious phallus. Also the ivory was very carefully etched with numerous tiny symbols. I say symbols quite deliberately for I am convinced that is what they were. They had significance. They meant something. On the island I saw enough similar symbols she made to convince me of this. They were more than patterns. They were language... written language!

Although I write this in the past tense, I still have that amulet and, in fact, it is around my neck even as I type these words. The old thong it was originally hung on dropped to pieces long ago and I now have it on a silver chain. I can sit look at it now and remember, as if it was yesterday, the day she hung it about my neck in great solemnity. It was a moment charged with significance and thereafter she would never let me take it off. I think it was her way of expressly taking me for her own. The meaning of those curious symbols etched on its surface, elude me yet with their message. It is a reminder that, as the days flowed into weeks and they in turn into months, I was only just beginning to come to know this remarkable woman.

Chapter Seven

One day (I suppose it must have been after I'd spent about two months on the island) I was down along the shoreline collecting driftwood. On these occasions I always kept my eye open for anything else that might be of any use and, this day, I had a real find. Washed up against some rocks a few yards off the beach was a large plastic garbage bin. An old discarded garbage bin might not seem anything to get excited about but it was as good as treasure from King Solomon's mines as far as I was concerned. There were literally dozens of uses we could put such a large receptacle to. My mistress was busy elsewhere on the island so I determined to recover that bin myself. I felt a thrill of pleasure at the delight she would show in my find.

I placed my driftwood carefully on a rock and set about formulating some sort of plan to drag that bin ashore. It wasn't easy for it was in an awkward place and there was some quite deep water separating me from the rocks it was jammed against. I had to wade in to a point where I was obliged to swim the last three or four yards to the rocks. As I've said before I was not a great swimmer, although I was improving under her example, but it was no great distance and the sea was flat calm. The major difficulty I had was in easing my way around the rock to the bin and then trying to shift it for it was mostly full of water and damned difficult to budge. After much labour and, after scraping my leg on the rocks, I managed to empty the water out of it and, using it as a flotation aid, I pushed off the rocks and kicked out for the beach.

I struggled ashore with it and then sat down on the beach to turn it over and gloat over my prize. To my delight there seemed to be no holes in it whatsoever. It was a real gem of a find. It was easily the largest container we possessed. I couldn't wait to show it to her.

It was while I was sat there, feeling so pleased with my discovery, that something caught my eye. I lifted my head to look and there, a mile or two offshore, a ship was passing. What I did next takes a little explanation and a good deal of understanding. I did nothing. I just sat there and watched that ship pass by and slowly fade into the distance almost as if it was an irrelevancy; something that belonged to another life I had somehow left behind. I didn't jump up and wave my arms or in any way attempt to attract the attention of that ship. My whole purpose at that moment was to drag that bin inland and present it to my mistress. I just sat and watched it sail away and, through that action, I demonstrated clearly how much I had changed.

I don't know quite when or by what stages I had come to this metamorphosis but I was a very different person now than the one who had futilely gesticulated at any passing ship in the early days of my confinement on the island. I suppose in the back of my mind there still remained some vestige of a consideration that I ought, some day, to think about being rescued: to think about returning to my own world and my own people but, somehow, such thoughts had become subsumed under the day to day realities of life with her on our island. The other world, that ship represented, seemed unreal now. My life was here and now on this island and, if I stopped to think about it, that was enough. In an odd way, and a way I would never have believed in my first days on the island, I was content.... more than that.... I was happy.

It might seem an incredible thing to claim. On the face of it I was imprisoned on a barren island by a creature who punished me at her whim or ruthlessly used my body for her sexual gratification. I was naked and so poor that an old discarded garbage bin seemed like treasure and living from day to day in a constant struggle for survival. By any sober analysis I should have been thoroughly miserable. Yet as I sat there on that beach I could honestly look within myself and realise that I had never been more contented and in harmony with the world about me in all my life.

I discussed this with a lady years later who is one of the very few people in which I've confided the true story of that summer. She suggested that I was showing evidence of the Stockholm Syndrome. This is, apparently, a paradoxical psychological condition where the victims of hostage situations grow to have empathy with and even affection to the point of defending the very people who are keeping them hostage. It seems the syndrome is named for a famous case where some bank employees were held hostage for a week by robbers at a bank in Stockholm, Sweden and came to be so close to their captors that they even defended them after they were released.

I am not convinced by this argument. My happiness went a lot deeper than merely some sort of misguided empathy with the person holding me captive. I genuinely felt a close affinity with nature; a kind of bonding with the world about me such as I had never experienced before. Somehow it took being naked and having nothing but my own wits to survive upon to really show me the things that were important in life.

Furthermore I was sharing that with a remarkable person. Close to her, I felt on the cusp of some deeper mystery; something of enormous importance to the whole meaning of human existence. I was in a privileged position, perhaps uniquely privileged, to observe at close quarters something completely outside of general human knowledge. There have been thousands of books written I suppose and endless hours of speculation about the possibility of intelligent life on other planets and what it might mean to us as human beings. The human species feels lonely. If there are other intelligent species out there, then we may not be alone in the cosmos. Well what if we are not alone even on this planet? What if there is another intelligent species on earth with which we could truly communicate with. Then we are not alone. I know we are not. I spent six months on an Aegean island proving that to my own satisfaction.

Chapter Eight

I lifted that garbage bin and went in search of my mistress as that ship vanished over the horizon. She was working at her shrine. I have to tell you about this shrine for it was one of the most mysterious and yet revealing things about her. I actually don't even know if it was a shrine but it always felt that way to me and that's how I always referred to it in my mind. It was a sort of small natural amphitheatre in the cliff on the side of the knoll. It looked like a small and old abandoned quarry to be honest and it may well have been the source of the material originally used to build the old villa at some time in the past. To her it had another significance however.

When not involving herself in the day to day business of keeping us both alive or spending her time abusing me for her pleasure she spent a lot of time working in that little quarry. Most of her labour there was completely incomprehensible to me though. She'd gouged out little niches and shelves along the rock walls and these she adorned with all sorts of decorations and oddities. Many of these just seemed purely decorative; odd coloured stones and seashells for example. She even placed odd bits of coloured plastic or metal, bits of broken crockery, old wiring... anything that took her fancy as pretty or colourful. One shelf held a collection of sea urchin shells, another, pieces of skeletons and dried plants and yet another pieces of broken tiling she foraged from the villa until she had all the walls of the quarry festooned with her treasures.

They weren't just randomly scattered about either. I've seen her agonising for hours over exactly where to place some particularly catching object; trying it in one place after another until she was happy with its placement. Once she was satisfied, that was where it stayed as well. She was very protective of that little spot. If I ever dared to move any of her adornments from its spot then I could expect a good spanking. She didn't even like me to touch them or go into the quarry when she was not there. I had to wait until she was out at sea fishing or something before I could go there and examine it at my leisure.

Most telling of all were the things she made to go in that place. She spent a lot of time carving things out of old pieces of wood or bone. These were often baffling for frequently they seemed to represent nothing identifiable. . mere abstract shapes. They must have meant something to her however for she devoted many hours of meticulous care to their carving. As I say, I had to wait until she was away fishing before I could examine these carvings of hers closely. To begin with I thought them just to be shapes that pleased her but one day I had an epiphany.

There was one largish display of pieces of carved wood and stones arranged together on a flat surface consisting of one large piece of intricately carved wood surrounded by smaller pieces of carving and pebbles. This display frankly baffled me and especially so because I knew of the care and attention she'd devoted to its arrangement. Yet it just seemed to be a placement of objects in some sort of pattern that appealed to her. I spent some time looking at this on this day and couldn't make head or tail out of it. Finally I abandoned the effort and walked up to the top of the knoll.

I used to do this every day for the knoll was the highest point on the island and, from there, you had a three hundred and sixty degree panoramic view over the whole island and the surrounding sea. I did this in the beginning to keep a look out for shipping but as the days on the island passed, and I came more and more to accept my situation, this became a lesser motivation. By now, I used the high elevation for instance to scour the sea for flocks of birds that might indicate schools of fish we might exploit. Also I used it to spot her. If she was late returning from fishing I'd be up there every half an hour or so sometimes worrying about her. You could often sight her out on the surface and she would frequently haul herself out on one of the rocks or tiny islets around the main island to groom herself or perform some other task. I was starting to get to know her favourite rocks especially the ones she sang from although that's a subject I'll return to.

Anyway, on this occasion, there was no sign of her but, as I scanned around, a blinding recognition flooded into my brain. The island and the surrounding rocks were laid out in a pattern exactly corresponding to the arrangement of objects laid out in the quarry. Excitedly I dashed back to the quarry to re-examine the arrangement. Now its significance was glaringly obvious. She had placed together a three dimensional representation of the island and surrounding features. It was a map. It was annotated too for many of the objects were marked with the curious interwoven patterns that I was coming to believe was her written language. She had even carved the large piece of wood to somewhat look like the island. You could recognise the knoll, the various bays and beaches and even the hollow with the villa and the olive grove.

I sat back on my haunches stunned by this unmistakeable evidence of her intelligence. This went way beyond the primitive carvings I had imagined. To carve or draw a likeness of something showed intelligence enough but it was familiar to our own prehistoric ancestors who painted pictures of animals, and so on, on cave walls. This showed a much more sophisticated relationship to her environment however. Again cartography is an ancient art among our species. I think they've identified crude maps dating back to some 25,000 years ago. I doubt if any of those maps showed such refinement and understanding as hers did though.

For one thing it was a three dimensional map and its spatial three dimensions did not end at the surface of the sea. Clearly shown on the arrangement were several submarine rock features around the island. I knew this to be the case for some of these rocks were easily visible beneath the surface in the clear water around the island. When I thought about it, I supposed it would be obvious that she would extend her cartographic record of the island below the surface of the sea. She lived in a three dimensional world above and below water level after all. When we make a map of a coastal area we normally use sea level as the boundary point and merely depict those features protruding above that. To her the boundary line was the sea bed or whatever depth of water precluded her from diving so deep. It was only late in our own history that we began to produce topographical maps of any description let alone those depicting submarine features.

It was yet another indication of both this woman's close affinity to us and at the same time the divisions that separated her from us. It was all too easy, as I hope I've made clear, to dismiss this woman as a naked primitive savage but then she'd show capabilities of such high intelligence that she could not only perceive the world about her in terms that seem foreign to most of us but also construct accurate topographical records of her perceptions for posterity.

Sat in that quarry with my mind reeling, I felt the hair on the back of my neck stand up. Suddenly that place was not at all what I had imagined it to be. I have called it a shrine, and perhaps it was, for it was a place of reverence and deep contemplation for her, but I began to see a far greater significance to it. Now, all of a sudden, it occurred to me that this was a place where she kept accounts. Many of the more baffling carvings or arrangements could be depictions of geographical features, some of them hidden beneath the sea's surface. The etchings on them, those enigmatic, infuriatingly elusive markings, could be annotations and descriptions. All the assorted objects gathered there could be an inventory; a collection depicting the rock types, marine life and anything else around the island all catalogued and cross referenced to its exact location.

Good God there was even a shelf on which she'd accumulated dried plants from the island. It might be a comprehensive survey of every type of plant on the island. The shells, crab skeletons and other remnants of sea life might be a catalogue of the marine life in the sea around us. If you understood the system in that quarry you'd be able to pick up a cockle shell from a shelf and instantly be able to identify, from its placement and accompanying description, exactly where it had come from and thus possess the knowledge to locate the beds of that particular species in the sea around. And I'd just thought they were pretty shellfish she liked the look of. The place was a journal... more than that... an archive; a record of her observations on and around that island.

And just how deep did that record go? Along one side of the quarry were a number of flat rock faces. She spent many hours meticulously carving her enigmatic messages into the surface of those rocks until it came that they were covered in those odd whorls and curved geometric patterns. If only I could have understood them. They might have been a written record of her time on the island... a very insight into her own thoughts and considerations. This woman was recording a history; a history of an intelligent species that was not our own. How might that have changed the world as we know it? What might we have learned from her?

There was one object in that quarry that held immense personal significance for her. I used to often spend time with her as she worked in her shrine and they were times of relaxation and quiet contemplation. I was always careful not to disturb the objects in the quarry but she liked to have me around as she worked at her carving or etching the rocks. I enjoyed watching her for she seemed at peace and contented in that place. Her hair would lie flat although it would sometimes quiver into life if something she was doing excited her. She'd squat there over her task, her ears twitching beguilingly and hum softly to herself or perhaps mumble to herself in her strange tongue. I think she derived great comfort from my presence for she liked to have me close and she'd frequently reach out to touch me or lean over and lick me.

One thing she never did however was mate with me in the quarry. This, in itself, was extraordinary because I doubt if there was a single other place anywhere on that island where she hadn't had her way with me. Her sexual appetite was so voracious and could manifest itself at any time that there wasn't a lot of ground we didn't cover. But that quarry was by and large the exception. I think this is what gave me the feeling that it was a place she revered and not to be sullied by her base desires. Of course while she was working there she would often put her chores aside and take a break by dragging me out of the quarry to ravish me somewhere but the quarry itself appeared to be sacrosanct.

This changed, however, on the day that she dedicated her most prized possession to the shrine within the quarry. It was a piece of amber. I know that amber is found washed up along shorelines so it shouldn't surprise me that she had a piece in her possession although I'd always understood that most amber is to be found along the shores of the Baltic Sea. It was, once again, a surprise however to find that she valued such semi-precious materials much as we do. Certainly she seemed fond of that piece of amber for she kept it in one of her little caches of treasures and she would often pull it out and finger it lovingly. I thought it was merely because she thought it pretty, which she undoubtedly did, but I didn't realise that she had plans for that piece of amber and, as she turned it over in her hands, she was equally turning over its possibilities in her mind.

After much cogitation she finally came to some sort of decision and she took the piece to the quarry and began very carefully to carve it. It was a sizeable piece of amber perhaps five or six inches long and maybe two to three inches wide and she took infinite patience with it. She used a variety of tools fashioned from metal which she doubtless accumulated in her foraging, including small files and an abrasive stone. In case you're not familiar with it, carving amber is a tricky and time consuming activity. It can be fragile and the trick is to remove only small amounts of material at a time. Also it is sensitive to heat so too much friction can cause it heat scars on it. The oddest thing about it though is a tendency for static electricity to build up in it which can cause it to fracture or chip when being carved or polished. Thus the way to handle it is slowly and with frequent pauses to allow it to cool down or lose its charge.

So she took enormous care over it and it was obvious that this carving was one of her most important projects and one which she was determined not to mess up. For a long time, then, it was difficult to know exactly what it was she was trying to carve from that piece of amber. When it did become apparent it took my breath away. Slowly, under her careful ministrations, the piece of amber began to take on the form of a figurine; a small statuette of a female form. She had carved the likeness of a woman and, when it was completed to her satisfaction and fully polished, it was a remarkably adept piece of craftsmanship; a beautiful tiny statue of a woman. It was the first thing I'd seen her make that was a recognisable image of a living thing. One thing was interesting about it. It showed a woman not a hermaphrodite. It was a depiction of my species not hers.

Delighted with it she shooed me away from the quarry and spent an afternoon with it on her own in the quarry singing. This was unusual for she mostly swam out to the outlying rocks around the island to sing. I've mentioned her singing before and it's worth elaborating on it at this juncture. Singing was another of her leisure activities you might say. Although she often hummed to herself while working a proper singing session was a rather formal and ritualised process. She had certain rocks jutting out of the sea which were her singing perches and she used these exclusively. She would most often adorn herself with her best ornamentation in the form of necklaces and bangles before singing and place ornaments in her hair or paint her body. It was something she generally dressed up for and I could always tell when she was setting off for one of her perches to deliver her songs.

I've said it before but it's worth repeating that I have never heard the like of her singing in all my days. There was an eerily evocative, almost hypnotic quality to those far carrying harmonies and melodies of hers and an underlying sense of some hidden depth to those incomprehensible, ululating arias. It was something almost magical and completely compelling. I'd sit on the beach and listen to her for hours with my spine tingling. It could be hours too for sometimes she could spend half a day or night singing from her rock. Whenever we had a full moon she would spend most of the night singing and I would huddle on the beach shivering and believe that I had never heard anything so strange or so beautiful in my life.

I don't know why she sang. It seems trite just to speculate that she did it simply because it gave her pleasure. There seemed far more significance in it than that or she would not have made such a formalised ritual out of it. I think there was definitely something territorial about it in that she sang to declare her ownership over her little realm in the same way a cock robin ritually takes to the same perches each day in his finery to claim possession of his little patch of garden or woodland with his song. I think that's only part of the story however. Certainly it was something important to her and it was a task she never neglected. There might have been some sort of religious motivation behind it although, in truth, I have no idea if she even had conceptions of religion that we might recognise.

But, on the occasion that she finished that amber carving, she broke with her usual formalities and sang from her quarry, shrine, whatever it was. I suppose she sang for two or three hours while I busied myself sorting out some tangles in our fishing lines. This was such a frustrating and niggling little job that I barely registered that she had stopped singing. Suddenly she appeared silently behind me. I jumped up from my task in surprise for normally she called out before coming looking for me. She held out her hand and obediently I placed my own in it. In rather solemn silence she led me back to the quarry.

It's difficult to describe what happened next for a lot of it I didn't understand. She spoke at length pausing often to touch me and lick me and I'm afraid I couldn't make any sense out of it whatsoever. She also spent some time bathing me with water she had fetched up in that garbage bin I mentioned earlier. She then dressed me in assorted ornaments she had made; necklaces, bangles and a string of seashells about my waist. All this was conducted in the greatest seriousness and I held my peace, somehow recognising the solemnity of the proceedings.

She seemed to go through a series of ritualised dances and postures and the little amber carving featured heavily in this for she carried it about often licking it reverently and smelling it. Finally she gave the little statuette a last lick and laid it carefully down on a sort of bed of soft dried grasses on a rock ledge, knelt down before it and sang some brief phrases. She then paused and looked at me curiously. I noticed that her penis was fully erect. "Somehow, don't ask me how, I knew what was expected of me. I came and knelt down facing the little carving with my back to her and bent forward, parting my legs, to present myself for her. She took me with what can only be described as gentleness by her standards and uttered a curious and strangely moving song as she did so. She ejaculated deep inside me but as she withdrew her copious flood of semen gushed from my vagina.

With deep reverence she scooped it up in her hands and smeared it both over me and the statuette. Felling that I ought to contribute something, I took some on my own fingers and followed her lead by wiping it on her body and the carving in equal measure.

The whole thing may sound ridiculous but, at the time, it felt very serious and deeply significant. The characteristic ambergris scent of her semen was heavy in the air. I've come to realise since that the choice of her material for the carving had another significance for her. Amber has a similar scent to ambergris, especially when burned and that may be the reason for the connection between the names amber and ambergris (which latter simply means grey amber). It was her sexual scent and, since I was pretty much covered in it twenty four hours a day, it was the scent she associated with me. Her little statue not only had a visual reference to me but also an olfactory one as well!

These formalities completed she sat on the ground and hugged me close for at least an hour crooning softly. Finally she licked me and took me by the hand and led me to the seashore. She supported me as she swam out to her favourite rock and helped me to climb up on it. Once we were perched on top she proceeded to sing for the next hour holding my hand all the time. I guess she was just registering me as her possession publicly. When she was done she carried me back to shore and we went about our business once more. But there'd been a subtle shift in our relationship. As I say I don't understand all about what happened during that ceremony but I have always since considered it to be my first marriage.

Chapter Nine

Life on the island was not without its problems. One problem that came to be critical was that of my diet. She might well have been able to live on a diet of fish and seafood but it was not a healthy balanced diet for me. I was losing weight. If any of you girls out there are looking for a good slimming diet I can recommend an exclusive diet of fish. It wasn't good though. I was by no means hungry but I was starting to look a little wasted and unhealthy. She seemed to realise this and she would often poke my body thoughtfully and seem concerned. Eventually she decided to do something about it and in a way that demonstrated not only her technical prowess but also a familiarity with my own kind that I had not suspected of her.

It was one day around I suppose the end of July although I was getting pretty vague about the calendar by this time. She'd spent a good deal of time fishing and brought so many fish ashore you'd have thought we were expecting guests. In fact she was just making sure that I had enough to eat for a couple of days because, after some preparations, she then vanished for over two days.

It was the longest she had ever been away up until then and I can remember how desperately lonely I felt. I was frightened that she'd just abandoned me and I spent the time pacing around the island and up onto the knoll to look out for her, feeling absolutely miserable. I even swam out to her favourite rock and spent an hour calling out for her at the top of my voice. I huddled in my bed in the ruined villa each night crying piteously and feeling more desolate than I had ever felt in my life.

She returned on the third day. I dashed down to the beach to greet her in unfettered joy. I didn't exactly run in circles around her, barking and wagging my tail but

you get the picture. She looked tired as well she might...
she'd had a hard couple of days. She was pleased to see
me however and not too tired to attend to immediate
domestic chores either for she was no sooner ashore than
she was making up for lost time and giving me the most
comprehensive boning she had yet subjected me to. I
didn't mind. I was pleased to see her too. It was pretty
characteristic of her. Any time that she spent a protracted
absence from the island her first priority upon returning
would be to give me what the Brits would call a damn
good shagging. I suppose there are worse ways to be
greeted upon one's master or mistress's return. Even the
lady that suggested I suffered from Stockholm syndrome
sounded kind of envious when I described this aspect of
my captivity. She'd been married for thirty years and I
guess she kind of counted her blessings if she got laid
more than about six times a year.

Anyway, having disposed of immediate
requirements, my newly returned mistress began to haul
her loot ashore. It took quite some time because she had
stashed it on an offshore islet a few hundred yards off the
beach. It was the first intimation that I ever had that she
possessed a boat. I guess if I'd thought it through
properly it was logical that she would have been able to
construct a boat. I think that she was such a phenomenal
swimmer it just never occurred to me that she might
need a boat of any description even if she possessed the
necessary technical know-how to construct one.. Well to
propel herself through the water she didn't need a boat of
course but that isn't to say that one was very useful.
There's only so much you can carry on your person
however formidable a swimmer you are and she was so
at home in the sea that the advantages of using
something floating to transport heavier cargo would have
been immediately apparent to her. Although I keep
pointing this out, she was intelligent, she spent her life in
the sea and she didn't think that human ships and fishing

boats were magic animals. Of course she had a boat.

It was a long time before she trusted me enough to let me see the little canoe she had hidden away on that offshore islet however. Perhaps she thought I might try to escape in it although I think the thought of setting out on a major sea crossing in that flimsy looking little craft would have scared the shit out of me. It was all right for her but I wasn't amphibious enough to take to the water if my boat decided to flounder beneath me.

If it was a revelation that she almost certainly had a boat then, as I watched her bring ashore the goods she had carried in it, there was an even bigger shock. She hadn't picked up her cargo from the open sea. Everything she hauled ashore had obviously come from some neighbouring island and, what is more, an inhabited neighbouring island. Doubtless some of the stuff she brought in had been foraged but even that was problematical. For instance she hauled a basket of oranges ashore. It was mid-summer. You grow sweet oranges through the winter and harvest them in spring so it was unlikely she just picked them off a tree. She had other vegetables and fruits outside of their growing season as well and, even more puzzling, a large ham and a string of those dried pork sausages the Greeks call loukaniko, which she obviously didn't find growing on trees. The heaviest object however was one which she ferried ashore from the islet on a plank of wood. It was a large sealed plastic sack of flour.

Now of course it was eminently possible that she'd sneaked ashore somewhere and stolen these goods. There must have been some sort of clandestine character to her foraging. I mean stark naked, amphibious hermaphrodites tend to raise eyebrows in shopping lines at the supermarket. Certainly she was stealthy enough and I pretty much already suspected her of relieving other inhabitants of the islands of their goods when opportunity arose. But nevertheless this seemed to

121

stretch criminal resourcefulness to a whole new level. I mean where do you steal a sack of flour from? Can you imagine how eerie it would be; the thought of some strange naked half-woman emerging from the sea by night to rummage about in your pantries and walk off with your sausages? You had the feeling the islanders would be locking their doors by night and offering up prayers to their local saints. I suppose they ought to be thankful that she wasn't carrying off their daughters and grateful that she had her work cut out looking after the one captive maiden she already had.

I wasn't convinced though. Romantic as the thought of my mistress pirating the local islands undoubtedly was, I had the sneaking feeling that it wasn't the whole story. I suspected immediately, and later would suspect it even more, that she had contacts with people; people with whom she traded. That brought up the disturbing thought that there were people in these islands who knew of her and her kind. It suggested that there were deep secrets among the Greek islanders; things that were not spoken about; perhaps contacts with these semi-mythical sea creatures that might go back many centuries in history and have spawned the innumerable stories of sea sirens, mermaids and other sea people of myths and legend of which the Aegean Sea is particularly rich in. She had the wherewithal to trade with the locals too. She was probably the best pearl diver in the entire Aegean basin.

But how did they communicate with her? Were there even people here that could understand some of her tongue? And then again would they not question why she wanted food stuff for a human person? Were there in fact people that knew or at least suspected that she had some person held captive somewhere? Was this another thing that was not talked about? Perhaps this kind of thing had happened before. There was something sinister going on here.

You don't know how much you miss bread until you don't have it. It's such a fundamental basic of life that you tend to take for granted. I once heard a biologist propound the theory that the dominant life form on the planet by biomass was in fact wheat. We just happen to parasite on it. Bread, at its most basic, is just flour and water with whatever else you care to chuck in it. It's more tedious hard labour than anything else but I had time on my hands and kneading dough made from that sack of flour kept me occupied while my mistress concerned herself with more important matters. I flavoured it with salt. If you're wondering where I obtained salt from then you're not thinking. We were surrounded by an ocean saturated in the stuff. I baked flat cakes of unleavened bread on hot stones in the fire and it was just heavenly. I even found that if you left a dough mix for some time it would leaven itself naturally with the natural yeasts in the flour. Of course we didn't have butter but by this time I was learning to make fish and seafood soups. Mopping it up with fresh bread seemed just luxurious.

It was good for me too. I'd been lacking carbohydrates and the other foods she brought back supplemented my nutritional requirements admirably. I wasn't exactly deficient in vitamin C. Fish isn't a very good source of this vitamin but it turns out that raw oysters are. In fact oysters are as good a source of vitamin C as lime juice. So I wasn't in imminent danger of scurvy because we often ate oysters but the citrus fruits were a welcome addition to my diet in any case. I began to put back on the pounds I had lost and started to look healthier.

As a result of this she made more frequent trips presumably to inhabited islands to obtain more food for me. One time she even came back with a dead lamb which I'm pretty sure she poached. We grilled it over the fire and it was the best feast I had on the island. Possibly irate shepherds have been wondering where their livestock has been disappearing to for millennia in the Greek islands and I know for a fact that she raided poultry as well.

There was one supplement to my diet that caught me completely by surprise however. One afternoon, following one of our regular couplings, she took a hold of me and pulled me to her breast. She held my face to her breast and pushed her nipple at my mouth. I thought that she just wanted me to suck on her nipple because she enjoyed it, so I complied. To my astonishment she was lactating. For several minutes she nursed me at her breast purring softly as I took her milk. I found it sweet and creamy and, oddly, I found it an entirely pleasant experience to nurse at her breast like a baby. I felt warm, comforted and somehow absurdly happy. I think I even fell asleep in her arms. Perhaps it was only a psychological bonding between us but after that she often nursed me and if, of course, she couldn't provide milk enough for an adult woman it was nevertheless a most agreeable intimacy.

Naturally I wondered how she could possibly be lactating for I'd always understood that lactation only occurs with the stimulation of pregnancy and child bearing. Since then I've done my research into the matter and it turns out that lactation is not at all confined to mothers. It is seen frequently in primitive cultures for example where women assume roles of surrogate mothers to children not their own. It is known from a number of other primate species as well and there seems to be some evolutionary survival advantages in populations with high maternal mortality. Even in modern women lactation can be induced by drugs or psychological stimulation in women that are not mothers. In fact I even learned that there is a whole field of eroticism around breast feeding adults and that continual stimulation of the breasts and nipples can induce lactation. There is even a name for a relationship between an adult couple in which one nurses the other or, in the case of lesbian relationships, mutual nursing. It's called an adult nursing relationship or ANR and is surprisingly common, especially among lesbians where it is a familiar expression of intimacy and tenderness.

For all that I thought that I knew everything about sex I was still pretty naive about some things in those days I suppose. That was one thing I learned from her and something I taught to another important person in my life that I'll tell you about later. I will say however that I came to love those tender moments suckling at her breast. I never felt more close to her than at those moments when she literally gave me the very substance of her body to nourish me and comfort me with. I think she loved it too for she'd purr softly and croon little murmurs that must have been endearments. It was at those times when I most felt that, in spite of the great biological divide between us, I loved this woman.

Chapter Ten

Perhaps it is my love for her that explains why, as that summer drifted along, that I abandoned the life I had once had and surrendered myself entirely to my existence with her on our tiny little island. There was a timelessness about the days as they melted one into the other; a seemingly endless sequence of enchanted days, bathing in the warmth of the Mediterranean sunshine surrounded by the azure waters of the Aegean Sea. My life before the island seemed unreal and mired in petty considerations that had no meaning here. It felt as if this was all life had ever been and would ever be again. But, of course, time does not stand still and as the days grew shorter the arrow of time was reaching out to pull me back to the world I had thought I had left behind for good.

Summer stretches long into the fall in the Aegean and if the nights were drawing cooler and the days shorter there was little indication that winter loomed as yet. It was well into October before I had any hint that my strange idyll on the island was coming to an end. I was down at the beach washing some root vegetables and herbs she'd brought back from her last trip when the world started to fall apart. I was singing happily to myself. She brought some squid ashore that morning and I was planning to make a calamari stew. She was eating more and more food that I cooked by now and I knew that she had a liking for the soups and stews I made. She was away at sea and I hoped to have it ready for when she returned. It would be a treat for her. I'd chosen to make my preparations on the beach where she most often came ashore so as to be there to greet her. She'd want me straight away after her labours and I'd save her the effort of coming looking for me. She could take me there on the beach and hopefully I'd have food ready for her as soon as she slaked her desire.

Then, very distantly, I heard her singing. I was puzzled for the song was coming from a long way away and she normally only sang from the rocks close to the island. There was something else too. The song had a different feel to it unlike her usual timbre. Curiously I laid aside my preparations and stalked up to the top of the knoll to see what she was doing. I could see no sign of her but the song fetched very faintly over the breeze from somewhere over to the west. I shaded my eyes against the glare and scanned the horizon but not a glimpse of her could I see. Then the song stopped abruptly and, with a shrug, I returned to my chores on the beach.

I had just stepped back onto the beach when she emerged from the sea expelling water from her gills. I froze at the sight of her, my spine tingling, for, in that moment, I knew that she could not have been the one singing so far away and now be here. That meant that it must have been somebody else; somebody else like her for no person of my kind ever sang like that. She was not alone. Somewhere, out to the west, was another of her species.

I think that she must have been underwater and failed to hear the song for she seemed no different from any other time returning from the sea. She had a sack full of shellfish in her hand, an erection in her groin and the familiar look in her face. I was trembling as I presented myself for her; not because I was frightened of her taking me but because of the implications of that distant song. She filled my womb with her semen and I licked the last drops from her penis as she liked me to do and then returned to my stew as she opened the shellfish. But I was distracted and my ears were alert in case that song should come again. But it didn't and by the time we had eaten, mated a couple more times and settled down into our bed in the ruined villa I was beginning to wonder if I had dreamt it after all.

I hadn't. The next morning I awoke to the sound of her singing. I walked down to the beach to bathe myself and squatted there to listen to her. She was sat on her favourite rock but her singing was different. She'd pause for long periods and during these periods I heard, somewhere far distant, an answering refrain. I shivered in fear as I listened to that unearthly exchange across the water and wondered what they were saying to each other and what it would mean for me. This went on for most of the morning and I huddled there miserably, instinctively knowing that somehow things would never be the same again.

When she swam back to the island she was agitated and paced up and down on the beach talking to herself nervously. How I wished at that moment that I could ask her what was happening or could understand what she was saying. For once she seemed too distracted to even mate with me and I simply sat and watched her fearfully as she seemed to struggle with her thoughts, pausing often to walk to the water's edge to stare intently out to sea. Finally she seemed to come to some decision. She strode up to me and grasped me tightly; just stood there and held me, for perhaps ten minutes or so, without a sound. Then, just as abruptly, she licked me once, relinquished her hold on me and waded out into the sea and vanished. It was the last I saw of her for the rest of the day.

That day seemed interminable. I thought she had gone for good this time. I thought another of her kind had called her away and she had gone. I felt so miserable that I could only pace around the island looking hopefully out to sea for her and crying. I had food enough but I couldn't bring myself to eat. I went and sat atop the knoll staring out to sea until the sun went down and the cool evening air drove me to my bed in the old villa where I pulled the old sacking around me and cried myself to sleep.

She returned in the middle of the night. I heard her step outside the villa and her scent preceded her as she squirmed into bed alongside me. I grasped hold of her crying in relief. She seemed puzzled by that for she licked at the wetness on my cheeks muttering oddly. I don't think she possessed tear ducts. I held on to her and wouldn't let her go for the rest of the night.

But things had changed. The next day she began to assemble her possessions and seemed to go through an inventory of them. She seemed oddly sad and listless however and stopped frequently as if lost in her own thoughts. I tried presenting myself and tempting her with my body but, for once, her libido seemed at a low ebb and she's just pat me and give me a squeeze before returning to her work distractedly. By the end of the day I had come to the inescapable conclusion that she was making her preparations to leave.

Chapter Eleven

Over the next few days her imminent departure became obvious. I didn't know what had passed between her and the other of her kind she had sung to but I guessed she must have swum out to meet whoever it was and that had decided her that she must leave. Perhaps it was a call to mate, perhaps it was time for her to migrate south for the winter. I just don't know. For all I know it might have been a call from her family or tribe. Whatever it was, it seemed imperative that she must depart although she looked anything but happy about it.

For the first time I saw her boat for she brought it from its hiding place on the big rock and grounded it on the beach where she began to laden it with her possessions. It was a remarkable craft; a long slim canoe fitted with an outrigger for stability similar to the sort I have seen since in the Polynesian islands of the Pacific and which I rather suspects come from the same technological culture. It looked well made and lovingly crafted but it seemed an awfully flimsy sort of craft to undertake any long sea voyage in. Then again, the Polynesians managed to undertake quite remarkable sea crossings in boats of no greater advancement and they didn't the supreme advantage that she had of not having to worry about drowning.

As she began to fill it up however the canoe looked awfully small; too small in fact for two people. I was already beginning to wonder what was to become of me and what she intended to do with me when the time came for her to leave. I suppose I was kind of hoping that she was going to take me with her; that we'd take her little canoe and sail off to new adventures over the horizon. It would be sad to leave the island however. It had become my home; possibly the only real one I had had since I left my parents' home in Iowa. Perhaps we were just sailing south for the winter. Maybe we'd return to our island in the spring and just carry on from where we'd left off. I didn't know but I watched her preparations with dread for the future.

She partially dismantled her shrine in the quarry, removing those objects of greatest value to her such as her carvings and other artefacts. The little amber figurine however she left until the last minute. She worked on other projects as well which she would not let me see and shooed me away if I tried to see what she was doing. Her preparations became more and more advanced and although she would break off to go fishing occasionally she was generally too engaged to spend much time with me or to do more than snatch a quick bite to eat. This doesn't mean that she neglected me. In fact during this period she probably showed me more real affection than at any other time during our relationship. It didn't comfort me for she'd hold me tightly and rock back and forth, crooning softly. I could feel her sadness. She was preparing to let me go.

At last the day came when her preparations seemed to be complete. She didn't leave straight away however. Instead she hung around the island for three days wistfully as if she could not bear to leave. She kept me at her side for the whole three days, stroking me and licking me sadly. Occasionally she took me but her heart wasn't in it and it seemed to leave her more disconsolate than ever. I was sad too. I knew she was trying to find a way to say goodbye.

At the end of the third day she surprised me again. Abandoning her boat and her possessions she dived into the sea and disappeared for two days. I knew she would return this time for she had not prepared so elaborately for her going as to leave all she owned behind. In spite of this I felt a great well of melancholy inside me, like a stone in my heart, for I knew instinctively that when she next returned it would be for the last time.

It was in the morning when she returned to the island and I was waiting for her on the beach. She took me then for the last time but it gave her no great joy. In the aftermath of that mating she took hold of me and held me and gave vent to a soft crooning moan that seemed to go on forever. It was her way of crying. I think her heart was breaking. She held me like that for at least two hours. I remember the tears running down my own face.

At length she rose and made a gesture for to me stay where I was. I obeyed and she walked sadly inland. I waited miserably but she soon returned and she had things for me. One was something I had even forgotten about. It was the sari I'd been wearing the day I fell overboard from the ship and she'd swum me to the island. She held it out to me and gestured that I should wrap it about myself. In puzzlement I did as I was told but it felt incredibly odd after all this time to cover my nakedness.

The next thing she gave me was valuable for it was a string of beautiful pearls that she'd drilled and threaded onto some old fishing line. She insisted upon tying this about me neck. There was some purpose in this gift I think for she touched it with her fingers and made a gesture imitating eating. I think she wanted to give me something of intrinsic value among my own people so that I could barter for food when she was not there to care for me. She was still looking after me you see.

The final thing she gave me was the little amber figure she had so lovingly carved. She licked it once and then pushed it into my hands. I couldn't stop crying. I have that little figure still. It is my dearest possession. I tell people that it is a piece of native art work I picked up on my travels. Very few know its true significance to me.

Curiously I had one thing to give her. It was a little gold ring that I'd worn all summer long; the only one of my possessions other than my sari that I had left after my debacle on the ship. It was only nine carat gold, quite plain and not very expensive but it was all I had to leave her to remember me by. It wouldn't fit on her fingers and she never wore rings anyway but she hung it solemnly on a cord around her neck and licked it tenderly.

After this exchange of gifts she held me long; licking at my face and sniffing at me as if to carry every last memory of my smell away with her. Then I became aware of an odd sound. It was a throbbing growling note. It seemed so strange and unnatural that I didn't recognise it. She knew what it was however for she licked me a last time and let go of me. Then slowly and sadly she waded out into the sea and vanished beneath the surface.

I stood there perplexed, looking at the point, where she had disappeared as the throbbing noise became louder. I shook my head and tried to make sense of what was happening. The sound rose in volume and then, to my astonishment, a small dilapidated looking fishing boat rounded the headland, the noise of its rickety engine defiling the tranquillity of the island. I didn't know how she had done it but I recognised immediately what she had done. She'd summoned somebody to rescue me.

In charge of this vessel was an old grizzled Greek fisherman and he eased the boat into the shore, pulling up against some rocks from where he beckoned me. My eyes blurred with tears I waded out to the rocks and he assisted me aboard. He nodded to me gruffly and said something in Greek I didn't understand before turning his boat around and pointing us back out to sea.

I stood in the stern of the boat gripping the rail in anguish as I watched the island grow smaller behind us. Then I saw her, sat atop her rock watching us leave. As I felt a wave of loss well up inside me she began to sing. The old fisherman busied himself with his wheel and gave no indication that he even heard her. I did hear her however and that last haunting melody will stay with me until the end of my days. There was such a melancholy in that voice that carried over the waves to me that I can close my eyes now and hear it still and it will still bring the tears that fell down my face then. Then it stopped and I lowered my eyes unable to bear the heartbreak any longer. When I raised my head again the rock was empty. She was gone. I never saw her again.

Chapter Twelve

The skipper of my boat was a man of few words it seemed for he maintained a taciturn silence as we sailed away from the island. I didn't mind the lack of communication. I huddled miserably in the stern of the fishing boat, lost in my own thoughts and hardly in a mood to talk. My tear blurred eyes were fixed upon the dwindling view of the island as we left it far astern. Soon it was nothing but a pinprick on the horizon and shortly afterwards I lost it in the afternoon haze. It felt as if something had been torn from my soul.

I blinked away my tears and glanced ahead. A sliver of land had appeared on the approaching horizon and, as the skipper pointed our prow in its direction, it seemed that it was our destination. I tried to shake off my melancholy and take an interest as the land grew closer. Soon I could make out details on the land. I could see buildings, whitewashed and clustered on a headland, and the masts of boats peeking over a harbour wall. I don't suppose we sailed much more than twenty miles but we'd crossed a dividing line between two worlds. Behind me was a dream, some eerie echo out of antiquity; primeval and evocative of lost memories. Ahead lay what we termed civilisation.

I was a different person now from that foolish little hippy girl that had fallen overboard all those months ago. This world ahead of me seemed alien and slightly frightening. I no longer felt I belonged in that odd world represented by those buildings and trappings of human society or the land before me. I wondered detachedly what would become of me there.

The skipper turned to say something to me but started and blushed before averting his gaze hurriedly. I was puzzled for a moment by his reaction. Then I understood. I'd tied my sari loosely in a knot around my breasts but it had slipped open from my waist and fallen away from my hips leaving me naked from the waist down. The poor man must have been horribly embarrassed. I'd grown so used to walking about naked it hadn't even occurred to me. I wrapped my sari about me more modestly and took stock of my appearance.

I must have been a strange sight. My hair was braided, held by a head band of old rope, and decorated with beads made of polished pebbles and seashells. I had bangles of seashells, urchin shells and sharks teeth on my wrists and ankles. There were odd symbols painted on my cheeks and forehead, a string of pearls threaded on old fishing line and my walrus ivory pendant around my neck. My amber figurine I clutched in my hand. I looked feral, almost savage; some primitive creature from before the dawn of civilisation. No wonder the skipper was reluctant to talk to me. They're superstitious in the Greek islands. I think he was afraid of me.

The skipper nosed his boat into the little harbour and tied us up alongside a stone jetty. He gestured at the jetty and mumbled something in Greek. I think he felt that he should assist me out of the boat but he was nervous of approaching me so I swung over the rail and stepped ashore unaided. The stone of the jetty was hot under my bare feet. I waited patiently while he secured his vessel and stepped onto the jetty beside me. He gestured hesitantly to bid me follow him and we walked ashore.

There were a pair of little cafes by the harbour side and there was a gathering of locals around the tables in front of them, sipping retsina and picking at bowls of olives. My appearance created something of a sensation. The locals scrambled to their feet and regarded this apparition with astonishment. There was a nervous babbling among them and I even saw a couple make the sign of the cross. I think if I had bared my teeth and hissed at them, in the way she did when she was annoyed, they would have scattered in panic. They must have thought that the fisherman Dmitri had pulled a wild mermaid in with his fishing nets.

When it became apparent that I wasn't going to bite or turn them into stone with a basilisk glare they recovered their composure and crowded around to stare and jabber excitedly among themselves. My rescuing skipper was surrounded and bombarded with questions. Before long people were emerging from houses along the quayside to see what the fuss was about and the crowd grew larger by the minute. In no time at all the whole scene had descended into the sort of richly comic drama that only the Greeks can stage manage. The discussion became more and more animated and it seemed impossible that anybody could hear anybody else over the cacophony. People were gesticulating wildly, calling on their saints to bear witness, arguing among themselves and beating their chests while I, the prize exhibit, stood in bewildered silence in the middle.

Dmitri the fisherman who brought me ashore was clearly somewhat agitated. I think he had instructions to take me elsewhere but the excited crowd around us was preventing him from doing so. He was shouting at people and growing red in the face but to little avail. Then somebody pushed a glass of wine into his hand and he became distracted. The crowd was getting bolder by the minute and one or two people (and I swear this is the truth) even reached out to poke me as if to reassure themselves that I was real. A little boy, he couldn't have been more than five or six years old, approached me with extreme caution holding out a bowl of olives like an offer of appeasement. I blinked in surprise but took the olives and nodded my thanks at which point he squealed in alarm and ran to hide behind his mother. I saw somebody emerging from the café with some more bottles and the crowd grew ever more argumentative and festive. I thought it a toss-up whether the whole affair would degenerate into a fight or a party, which, in Greece, often amounts to the same thing. Just then, however, authority arrived.

Authority was not a reassuring sight. Authority was represented by a short but stout, florid faced policeman stomping down the cobbled quayside, puffed up with self-importance and sweating copiously under his crumpled and ill-fitting uniform. His appearance on the scene elevated the drama to even greater heights of farce. He seemed to have taken it into his head to take Dmitri's extraordinary passenger into custody as possibly a dangerous alien. The crowd seemed outraged by this and, with a single unintelligible voice, began to take issue with him. Dmitri was particularly incensed and, before long, he and the policeman had squared up to each other, bawling at the top of their voices and shaking their fists in each other's faces while the rest of the crowd stood on the side-lines inflaming the standoff in a quarrelsome babble. I didn't know whether to laugh or cry. Greek, by the way, is one of the richest tongues on earth to curse in and doubtless there were superbly earthy epithets turning the air blue.

Eventually the policeman's authority gained the upper hand, assisted by the truncheon he was threatening to brain Dmitri with, and before I knew it a handcuff had been clamped on my wrist and I was being led away into the village. The local crowd however was not prepared to let matters rest at that and we were accompanied by the whole lot of them forming a volubly arguing procession through the village being joined at every house by newcomers. By the time we reached what passed for a police station I think we must have had the entire village in tow. I didn't know whether it was a revolution or a lynch mob.

I was pushed hastily into the police station and I could hear muffled bangs against the walls. I think the mob outside was throwing stones at the place. I was unceremoniously ushered into a small dingy office which was sweltering and inadequately cooled by an old-fashioned ceiling fan which was turning lazily above and emitting alarming wheezes and groans as if the motor was on its last legs. There were flies buzzing about in the office and there was a gecko clinging to the ceiling. I was bade to plant my rear on a rickety wooden chair facing a cluttered desk and the officious little arresting officer took up station on the far side of the desk and began to interrogate me.

To be honest I think that the policeman, having won custody of me over the protests of the assembled villagers outside, was now at a loss about what to do with me. It helps, of course, when interrogating an American citizen, to have more than a rudimentary command of the English language, which my captor sadly did not. I managed to give him my name and nationality and after that we more or less hit an impasse. He kept demanding my passport. Now since all I was wearing was a flimsy little sari, which barely covered me with any modesty, I can't imagine where he thought I was concealing my passport. I kept trying to tell him that I'd fallen overboard from a ship but he didn't seem to grasp the point.

He did take a great interest in the pearls around my neck and the amber figurine I was carrying. Maybe he thought I'd stolen them. He wanted to take them off me but when he tried I snarled at him. I mean I literally snarled at him. I guess I'd been living the feral life for too long and gotten used to expressing myself appropriately. Whatever the reason it scared the hell out of him. I was only a little slip of a thing but I was a wild girl by now and I wasn't going to let this pompous little jackass piss on me. He didn't try to touch my possessions again.

I demanded to be allowed to contact the US

embassy but he seemed to think that was an insult to Greek pride and he pounded his fist on the table and growled something unflattering about President Nixon. Well I grew up among South Iowa farming country so I knew a bit about how to cuss too. After an hour or so of getting nowhere and trading insults we were reduced to glaring at each other across the table while the crowd outside grew more rancorous by the minute. I guess they'd been sending delegations back to the café for more wine to fuel the insurrection. I was half expecting them to storm the police station.

The deadlock might have continued indefinitely had salvation not turned up at that point. The crowd outside grew suddenly subdued and a minute or so later a gentleman strode into the police station. This was how I met Doctor Stephano Theodorakis, the second most remarkable person I encountered in my Aegean adventure. It was apparent, from the moment this gentleman marched into that office, that here was the real authority on this island. He was a tall man dressed immaculately in a pale grey suit, impeccably polished black shoes and black neck tie. He carried a Homburg hat in one hand and an ivory topped, black cane in the other. He was middle aged and greying but his grey eyes sparkled with good humour and gentleness. He had a meticulously groomed goatee beard and carried himself with quiet dignity and self-assurance. He was, I was to learn, that rare species, a true gentleman; always impeccably dressed, immensely charming, kind and invariably courteous. He was the true patrician on that island and the one person to whom everybody locally would defer to in respect. He was also, I was to learn in time, possessed of one of the most brilliant scholarly minds I have ever come across and his self-effacing modesty masked an almost encyclopaedic knowledge of whatever subject you cared to engage him in conversation over. This was the man who would come in

140

time to be one of my dearest friends and my most lasting inspiration.

Chapter Thirteen

The appearance of Dr Theodorakis completely took the wind out of my belligerent little interrogator's sails. The policeman jumped to his feet and, while he didn't exactly touch his forelock in servility, his earlier self-importance wilted visibly before the dignified authority of this gentleman. There was a short exchange between my captor and Dr Theodorakis and the policeman wrung his hands nervously as the doctor quizzed him calmly. It seemed that my rescuer had demands of his own and he delivered those demands with quiet assurance. In all the time I knew Dr Theodorakis I never once heard him raise his voice. His requests however were decisive. The policeman was nodding obsequiously in agreement and babbling his submission to this gentleman's authority. With reserved satisfaction, the Doctor turned to me.

"Please excuse my incivility Miss. Am I correct in assuming that I am addressing a Miss Delilah Delmonte of Iowa in the United States of America?" The voice was deep, beautifully modulated and assured; the English flawless and with the barest hint of an accent.

I blinked in surprise. "You know my name?"

"Ah so I am correct. Forgive me Miss Delmonte. I have er... made inquiries in the last few days as to your possible identity. I discovered that a young American lady of that name was reported as missing last May and, since the constable here has confirmed that you are indeed American, I deduced that you must be that same young lady."

"Why sure... that's me."

The gentleman held out his hand. "Then I am most pleased to meet you Miss Delmonte. I am Dr Stephano Theodorakis at your service." I took the proffered hand in confusion and he bent over it in a short grave bow. "I do hope you will forgive me for this inconvenience Miss

Delmonte." He continued. "Dmitri, the fisherman, was supposed to deliver you directly to my own residence but he seems to have been a little remiss in the execution of his instructions and allowed himself to surrender custody of you to our local police authority. However, I have managed to persuade the constable here that you are not a criminal and that your interests would be better served by releasing you into my care until such time as we can inform the appropriate authorities that you have been found and can deliver you safely back to your loved ones and family."

I stared at the gentleman in astonishment. "Did you send that fisherman to fetch me here then?" I demanded.

"Yes Miss Delmonte. I er... I thought it best under the circumstances. I would like to extend to you the hospitality of my house until we can reunite you with your family. I think you will find it far more agreeable than the police station and I'm afraid this is only a small island and we have little in the way of suitable hotel accommodation for a young lady."

"So how long have you known I was on that island?"

Dr Theodorakis looked uncomfortable. "Only latterly I'm afraid Miss Delmonte. I have suspected for some time that somebody had er... taken up residence on one of the uninhabited islands nearby but I have only of late come to learn that it was a young lady and, as I have mentioned, it is only in the past few days that I have come to any theory as to the identity of that young lady."

I swallowed as the implications sank in. "Did... did she tell you that I was there?"

Dr Theodorakis looked grave but slightly evasive. "I think, if you'll forgive me Miss Delmonte, that er... these are matters best discussed privately. Suffice it to say that I have had some contacts with your... er your late companion and that those contacts have been instrumental in determining my course of action.

143

Possibly it was remiss of me not to have accompanied Dmitri in recovering you and I might have saved much inconvenience and embarrassment had I done so. I thought however to be discreet and Dmitri assured me that he would bring you ashore without any due fuss. Sadly my plans seem to have unravelled somewhat. Possibly I should have realised that it is nearly impossible to exercise discretion on such a small island. I'm afraid I was never very good at this cloak and dagger sort of thing."

"So you... you could talk to her?"

Dr Theodorakis bit his lip thoughtfully. "Again I must say Miss Delmonte that these are matters best dealt with in confidence. If you would afford me the signal honour of accompanying me to my house I will be able to answer your questions at our leisure. I have had a room prepared for you and doubtless you would be grateful for some sustenance following your travails of today. Also I have instructed my housekeeper to acquire some clothing suitable for a young lady. Charming though your present attire is, I'm afraid it may raise eyebrows among our conservative local populace and also the evenings are getting rather cool at this time of year and I'm sure you would be thankful for somewhat warmer clothing."

Well, when he put it like that, there was really no question of any other course of action. I didn't take to the idea of spending a few nights in a cell in that dilapidated police station and this calm, dignified gentleman seemed a much better champion of my cause than a fat, sweating and obstreperous policeman. There was something very paternal about Dr Theodorakis; something that made you feel safe and protected. Throwing myself on his mercy was an easy decision and, unlike my previous guardian, he was not the kind of man to take advantage of my reliance on his generosity. He never treated me with anything other than courtesy, deference and scrupulous correctness.

Once we had paid homage to necessary formalities and divested ourselves of my fat policeman, Dr Theodorakis led me out of the police station. There was still a considerable crowd outside but they had fallen into a respectful silence in deference to the Doctor's presence. Waiting for us on the cobbled street was a little two wheeled pony trap to which was harnessed a phlegmatic and rather shaggy looking pony waiting patiently in the shafts. Mounted on the Dickey box at the front was no other than Dmitri, my erstwhile rescuer from the island, who seemed to perform a multi-functional role in the Doctor's employ. Whilst the crowd stood around watching respectfully, Doctor Theodorakis solemnly assisted me into the trap. I felt like a rather savage and exotic princess being paraded in front of the locals.

Throughout our drive to the Doctor's house we remained silent for the most part. I fingered my amber statuette somewhat nervously and it caught the Doctor's eye. "Forgive me Miss Delmonte," he said. "I could not help noticing that small figurine you are carrying. Am I right in assuming that it is some token of... of your late companion?"

"Yes... yes she made it and gave it to me."

"May I be permitted to look at it Miss Delmonte?" Nervously I handed it over. Doctor Theodorakis seemed entranced by it. He examined it minutely and ran his long slender hands over it lovingly. "Remarkable, quite remarkable." he murmured to himself. He handed it back to me reverently. "You must take great care of that Miss Delmonte." He told me gravely. "It is an extremely rare and most precious artefact."

I clutched my statuette to my breast protectively. I fixed my gaze on him intensely. "What do you know of her sir? You do know about her don't you?"

Doctor Theodorakis sighed and nodded gently. "Yes

Miss Delmonte. I know something of her and of her kind. I fear though that my knowledge is very incomplete. I have made something of... of... well a study of her kind but there is a great deal that I don't know. I shall be most interested to hear your story Miss Delmonte if you would be kind enough to confide it in me. You would do me a great service if you were to help me fill in some gaps in my understanding. Such a close and intimate contact which you appear to have enjoyed with your companion would, I think, provide remarkable insights into an extraordinary and virtually unknown people. In return I can tell you the little I know of her and her people."

"What sort of people are they?" I asked.

Doctor Theodorakis glanced uncertainly at the stolid figure of Dmitri driving the trap. "I think perhaps our conversation should wait Miss Delmonte. Would you please be patient a little longer?"

I nodded. "If you wish Doctor but I want some answers. Things happened to me on that island and I've seen things that I don't understand. I want some answers to them."

Dr Theodorakis nodded in acknowledgement. "I shall endeavour to tell you what I know Miss Delmonte but perhaps it would be better to wait until we have seen to your more immediate requirements. After we have seen to your accommodation and suitable attire perhaps you would do me the honour of dining with me. After we have dined we can talk at greater length. I think matters of importance are best discussed on a full stomach. Tomorrow we must endeavour to make contact with the authorities on the mainland and your embassy to inform them that you are alive and well. I should imagine that your family will be extremely happy to hear that you are safe."

I blinked back my tears, torn by conflicting emotions. I realised that my family probably thought that

I was dead. I missed them but I missed her too. "Yes," I whispered quietly. "I guess they will be."

The Doctor's house was about half a mile away; a large and beautiful white villa set among cypress trees a little back from the track that passed as a road. It was an old and eccentric house of solid stone and whitewashed plaster, roofed in red tiles in classical style and with curious outbuildings and extensions. It was charming and cosy looking although large enough to be regarded as opulent and it was in fact the largest private dwelling on the island. It was rather like Dr Theodorakis himself in fact; immaculate yet reassuring, dignified yet comforting and modest while at the same time carrying the weight of authority. This was a house where you knew instinctively that the owner was both unostentatious and at the same time the most important person on the island.

I was ushered into the house with great dignity and handed over to the mercies of Isadora, Dr Theodorakis' energetic and garrulous housekeeper. This little whirlwind bustled me away jabbering away to me, completely oblivious, seemingly, of the fact that she spoke no English and I couldn't understand a word she said. In spite of the communication difficulties however she took great care of me. Within half an hour of arriving at the house I was enjoying a luxury that had been beyond the dreams of avarice for the entire duration of the summer... a hot bath. I settled blissfully among the suds. Civilisation had its compensations it seemed.

Isadora had a loose interpretation of the meaning of privacy for, as I lay in the bath, she burst into the bathroom, without the formality of announcing her entrance with a knock on the door, and began laying out clothes for me. The clothes were a bit challenging. She laid out a sort of chemise and bloomers in white, long white stockings, a long skirt in dark blue accessorised by a spotless embroidered apron and the traditional Greek

147

ladies' blouse in white cotton embroidered with blue floral trimmings. There was even a pair of leather buckled shoes that fitted me well enough. I brushed out my hair and tied it in a ribbon and stood in front of the bathroom mirror to admire myself. I quite liked the look, now I'd managed to dress myself. Twirling in front of the mirror I looked just like a Greek peasant girl dressed in her Sunday finest.

I was given a room with a window view overlooking the sea, for Dr Theodorakis' house sat in a pleasant situation by a small bay. The room was old fashioned even back then in the seventies, with an enormous brass bedstead covered in brightly coloured quilts, fancy lace curtains over the tiny windows, thick woollen rugs over bare floorboards and simple wooden furniture. There were flowers in a vase on a small table and a couple of oil paintings of the Greek islands hanging on the walls. There was a book on the bedside table. I couldn't read it, for it was in Greek, but I recognised it; Homer's Odyssey.

After I was refreshed and suitably attired, I was left to my own devices for a while. I sat on the edge of the big bed and tried to come to terms with my new world. I wasn't left to brood for too long however. There was a discreet knock on the door and I opened it to be confronted by a small, dark haired but dignified man that turned out to be Milo, Dr Theodorakis' butler and general manservant, who, in passable English, informed me that the Doctor hoped that I was rested and refreshed and requested, if it was not too onerous an obligation, that I join him for dinner.

I was almost intimidated sitting down for dinner with Dr Theodorakis. It wasn't the Doctor's fault for he was exceedingly courteous and deferential. It was just that months of living a feral life on the island had left me ill-equipped to deal with the trappings of civilised behaviour. We were sat at opposite ends of a long, polished walnut table, elaborately decorated with silver platters, candelabra and floral displays. My place setting held a decorative table mat, an imposing array of high quality silver cutlery and a spotless white linen napkin held in a silver napkin ring. I'd spent most of the last six months eating with my fingers. Even the soups and stews we'd made on the island I'd scooped up with bits of bread or sipped straight from the battered old pan we'd used. I felt sure I was going to disgrace myself.

My misgivings were somewhat ameliorated by the excellence of the food. Dr Theodorakis had a most gifted cook and one who presumably thought that I must be verging on the point of starvation after my ordeals, judging by the amount of food that was laid before me. There was a hearty and nourishing fasoulada to begin with, which is a sort of traditional Greek soup made from white beans, vegetables and olive oil. This was followed by a horiatiki salad of cucumbers, tomatoes, green peppers, red onions, feta cheese and kalamata olives all dressed in lemon juice and olive oil and accompanied by crusty rustic bread and a side dish of tzatziki. Then there was a fish dish of baked sardines seasoned with pepper and origami and drizzled with lemon juice. The main course was a delicious, traditional moussaka; layers of aubergines and minced meat, topped with a white sauce and baked in the oven. Just in case there were any lingering traces of malnutrition we finished off this largesse with something with the horrible name of galaktoboureko, which proved to be a heavenly baked dessert of semolina and egg custard drizzled in melted butter and flavoured with vanilla, a collection of gooey Greek pastries and dark thick Turkish coffee. This feast was laid before us by Milo and a young serving girl with a cheeky twinkle to her eye who was on a mission to get me pie faced judging by the amount of times she insisted on topping up my wine glass.

After this repast I could have pretty much crawled away to hibernate somewhere but Dr Theodorakis courteously invited me to join him for a digestif of Metaxa brandy in his study.

The Doctor's large study was his inner sanctum and the most revealing chamber in the house of the character of this remarkable gentleman. There were huge, comfortable, leather upholstered armchairs, uncompromisingly masculine and solid, in front of a large log fire. The walls were covered in cabinets and an extraordinary collection of bookshelves. This man was a serious scholar. There must have been thousands of books in there, many of them beautifully bound with gilt lettering on the spines glinting in the subdued light of the lamps and fire. There was a huge mahogany desk cluttered with documents, artefacts, an old fashioned brass microscope, mathematical instruments, magnifying glass, a curious looking device which I learned later was a Van der Graff generator and, of all things, a stuffed weasel.

Those spaces on the walls not covered in bookshelves held a fine collection of art works and there were classical busts set into alcoves. Other tables held glass laboratory equipment, collecting jars, a butterfly net, collections of dried plants, dissecting tools, model ships, samples of minerals, a glass tank containing wall lizards and, curiously enough, a partly stripped down, Colt 45 revolver. In one corner stood an easel and artist's tools and there was a huge brass telescope mounted on a tripod at the big bay window. This man was a polymath in the great nineteenth century tradition; a man who turned his restlessly enquiring mind to almost anything.

We settled down in the big armchairs by the fire and the Doctor filled a well-worn briar pipe with tobacco and infused the atmosphere with aromatic fumes. I don't smoke myself and I generally dislike having to inhale people's tobacco smoke but the earthy rich scent mingling with the aromas from the fire was entirely appropriate to the masculine comfort of that fascinating room and the paternal presence of the man whose domain this was. Sipping my fiery brandy and toasting in front of the crackling fire I felt warmly secure and oddly comforted. Dr Theodorakis would always be a sort of father figure to me and, even years later when I was a mother myself, I would always feel like a little girl at her father's feet in his wise and gentle presence.

We talked long into the night. It was the most extraordinary conversation of my life but some of my recollections of it are a bit vague. I was replete with food and, after long abstinence, I was unused to alcohol so I guess I was a bit sleepy to begin with. It was nevertheless an illuminating and thoroughly thought provoking conversation and one which change my life forever.

Chapter Fourteen

We started with my story. Dr Theodorakis wanted to hear everything that had happened to me from the moment that I set foot in Greece to my arrival on his doorstep. I told him everything; every last detail of my time on the island. It was cathartic for me to recount my tale and he listened in rapt interest, interrupting me from time to time to clarify certain details or to ask pertinent questions of my observations. His grey eyes gleamed as I told my story and he nodded in sage satisfaction; as clear a sign as you could have hoped for, given his reserved nature, that he was fascinated and excited by my story. He made me go over parts of my story again and again, expanding on every minute facet; no detail too trivial for his inquiry.

He wanted to know everything about her; every way she fished or hunted, her ornamentation, what I could recall of her songs and vocalisations, how she swam, details of her anatomy, what sort of tools she used, how her boat was constructed, how she made fire or prepared food and any number of other things. Many of the details I furnished him with he seemed already to know and merely nodded as if I was just confirming his own observations. Some things were quite clearly revelations to him however. He became visibly excited when I told him about her shrine in the old quarry and the artefacts and inscriptions she had made there. He made me describe them time and time again, omitting no detail that I could recall, and his eyes sparkled with profound interest. He rubbed his chin ruefully. "My word! I wish now that I'd accompanied Dmitri to the island. This is remarkable! You say that the contents of that quarry are still there?"

"Most of it sure. I guess she loaded most of the most intricate small carvings and valuable things into her boat but a lot of it must still be there and of course the inscriptions on the rock faces must still to be seen."

He slapped a fist into his palm. "I must venture out there and see for myself. Certainly I must have photographs for posterity. There could be a treasure trove of information in those inscriptions alone. Have you any idea how important they could be? It could represent a breakthrough in our understanding! I have only ever come across tiny fragments of inscribed objects before and I've never come close to transliterating them. You say she annotated three dimensional cartographic representations?"

"It seemed so to me sir. I could be wrong of course."

My dear God! I hope those annotations are still there. If you are right Miss Delmonte they could be the key to deciphering her written language. We may have uncovered the means to trace her very history and that of her people. Tell me. You say that she had her collections ordered in some specific way?"

"Oh sure. It was kind of like she had them arranged in logical order; almost catalogued."

"Remarkable, remarkable! Please elucidate Miss Delmonte." And so I did while he sat with his fingertips pressed together as if in prayer, a characteristic pose of his, and nodded encouragingly with his warm grey eyes gleaming keenly with interest.

At long length I ran out of steam and fixed him with an enquiring gaze. "So what do you make of all that sir?"

He didn't answer immediately. Instead he pushed another log onto the fire and refilled our brandy glasses before settling back in his armchair and closing his eyes in cogitation for a few moments. Finally he sighed and shook his head. "I scarcely know where to begin Miss Delmonte. I must say that that is the most extraordinary story I have ever heard. I must say that I envy you Miss

Delmonte. Few people nowadays have such an opportunity to live in such close daily intimate contact with one of your companion's kind. I believe it happened more often in antiquity but such occurrences are rare indeed now. There were one or two rumoured instances of such cohabitation from before the last war and several I believe in the last century. There have been stories in the islands of people being abducted and held by her kind throughout history of course and there are innumerable references to aquatic hominids in mythology."

I shook my head decisively. "There was nothing mythological about her." I declared.

"Quite Miss Delmonte. Both you and I know that she and her kind do exist. We are among the few remaining people privileged to have observed her people at close quarters."

"How do you know of her folk sir?"

Dr Theodorakis took a deep breath. "I first came upon the sea people when I was a young boy Miss Delmonte. I had a boat that my father built for me and I would spend all my summer days out on the sea exploring all the islands within the range of my boat. Among those islands I came into contact with the same people you have described."

"I think there were more of them in those days for I encountered at least half a dozen individuals quite regularly among some of the more distant islets from here. I wasn't alone in that. A number of the older people used to talk about the sea people as they called them although it was never something that was discussed openly for people were frightened of them and considered them to be harbingers of ill fortune. There were one or two remote islands that had a reputation for being frequented by them and the superstitious fishermen would go nowhere near them. The elders here would have been horrified to know that I came into contact with them. They were said to steal young boys and girls. I learned to keep quiet about my trips to see them for I would certainly have been forbidden to do so had anybody known "

I found I was holding my breath. "So you've met them often?"

"Not so much in recent years Miss Delmonte but I certainly encountered them on many occasions when I was young. There was one island where I frequently saw them. The first time I saw them I was drawn to the island by hearing one of them sing, in the way that you've described, from the rocks. I was rather frightened I confess but I rowed my boat among some rocks to hide and listened for a long time, peering fearfully at this incredible creature perched on the rocks and serenading the sea with its haunting melodies."

Dr Theodorakis chuckled to himself. "She knew I was there of course. I don't think much escapes them in their natural environment. I think they were a little wary of me to begin with but after a while they seemed to tolerate my presence. Gradually I gained their trust and they would come right up to my boat. I used to bring them gifts. I found that they particularly valued things made of metal.; copper, aluminium, tin and, most particularly iron and steel. They greatly prized knives of any description or any steel tools."

I laughed shortly. "I can relate to that. Knife blades were like gold to her."

Dr Theodorakis nodded sagely. "Yes indeed. Before I'd set off on an excursion to the island I'd load my boat up with all sorts of gifts; old penknives, axe heads, fishing hooks, needles, old pots and pans, harpoon heads such as our fishermen used to catch octopus with, old tin cans and scrap metal. They would take it all. It wasn't just functional objects they valued either for I sometimes brought them food stuffs and decorative items such as glass beads and marbles, porcelain figures, little metal

155

painted toys or enamelled bits of cheap jewellery... anything bright and pretty. In return they'd fetch me fish they'd caught or lobsters and clams. They even gave me pearls and valuable minerals they'd collected. I kept them to myself but the fish I brought back for the household, I told my parents that I'd caught myself." Dr Theodorakis paused to chuckle fondly. "I suppose that I ran an interspecies trading business. I was very young of course and it all seemed like a great adventure at the time" He shook his head sadly. "It didn't last naturally... well not to the same extent anyway."

"Why? What happened?"

"The war of course. Italy invaded our country in 1940. That was not so bad for our army pushed them back into Albania but the Germans intervened in the spring of 1941 and within two months we were defeated and under Axis occupation. After the fall of Italy in 1943 our whole country came under Nazi occupation. They were hard years in Greece Miss Delmonte. The Germans were cruel and there was much oppression and deprivation. Fishing was banned throughout the Aegean as was most unauthorised marine traffic. I could not go to sea in my little boat for fear that the German patrols would fire on me. I heard rumours that the Germans had fired on small canoes, much like the one you have described, for they feared the infiltration of Allied commando raids and the resistance. Perhaps they drove the remaining survivors of the sea people out of the Aegean for they became even scarcer and more elusive than ever. For many years I heard of no reports of them at all. I began to worry that we had seen the last of them and that no record would remain in human knowledge bar the whisperings of folk tales and ancient myths."

Dr Theodorakis paused sadly to refill his pipe before continuing. "I was unduly pessimistic Miss Delmonte for, while they became very elusive and wary, some vestiges of their people survived the war years. I came upon them very seldom but it seems there had been some favourable memory of me among them. I suppose I had gained their trust and goodwill for, after some years, I had some further contacts with them. They would visit this island here in great secrecy to trade with me for certain goods that were precious to them.

I had inherited this house and my parents' estate by then for my father died during the war, my mother passed away in the fifties while I was attending university in Athens and I was an only child. I returned to the island of my birth and took up residence here and, very slowly, I began once more to renew my acquaintance with those strange people who had so fascinated me as a boy and teenager before the war. Their visits to me were always very clandestine and infrequent. Sometimes many months or even years would pass without my seeing any of them and I never came to know more than a handful of them. As the years passed their visits became more and more infrequent until, some seven or eight years ago they ceased altogether. I thought then that I had lost contact with them forever."

Dr Theodorakis seemed lost in melancholy for several seconds as the memories passed through his mind. Finally he collected his thoughts and continued. "It became my life's work to study and learn as much as I could about those people. I travelled extensively throughout the Mediterranean searching for evidence of them. I interviewed old peasants, fisherman and sailors, anybody who might have old recollections or might have information. I visited numerous islands where there were reputedly sightings of them. I scoured old mariners' records for references to mermaids or sea nymphs. Fortunately I could disguise my researches for I was by now a respected authority in mythology. Few among my academic colleagues suspected that my interest in such tales was anything more than a curiosity in the origins of mythology among folk tales."

"Everywhere Miss Delmonte I came upon tantalising clues and infuriatingly elusive accounts of contacts with these people. There were mariners' stories long dismissed as the over excited imagination of sailors that have been at sea too long. There were myths among isolated island dwellers stretching back into antiquity, tiny glimpses of the truth among primitive peoples that lived along the ocean fringes and the banks of great rivers and a wealth of legends and stories from among nearly every society that lived in close harmony with the sea."

"Among my own people, of course, there are innumerable myths and legends of fantastic creatures and it would be easy to dismiss the many references to aquatic humanoids in Greek mythology had one not the personal experience that such people really existed. There were the sirens of antiquity that were said to lure sailors to their islands with their fantastic songs and who were said to be the daughters of the God Achelous. Some Roman poets even cited a group of islands called the "Sirenum scopuli" as the dwelling place of the sirens. In Greek folklore the sirens were fully aquatic human creatures and the name for a mermaid in many European languages is interchangeable with the word siren; Sirena in Spanish, Sirene in French, Sirena in Italian and Portugese. Even Polish and Romanian use the word siren for a mermaid. We derive the name for the order of marine mammals known as sea cows and includes the dugong and manatees from the word, for their Latin collective name is Sirenia."

"But they are certainly not the only aquatic human like creatures in Greek mythology." Dr Theodorakis pointed out, as he warmed to his theme. "Of particular interest are the Nereids, the sea nymphs who were thought to be the daughters of Nereus and Doris and frequently accompanied the sea god Poseidon. These were important minor deities among the Aegean islands for they were the patrons and protectors of seaman and fishermen. They were supposed to live in a sea cave in the Aegean with their father and there were said to be fifty of them although over ninety are named in ancient Greek sources. They are usually depicted as beautiful women, frequently riding on the backs of dolphins."

I gave a snort of laughter at this point. "That figures."

Dr Theodorakis chuckled in agreement. "Yes indeed Miss Delmonte. Much the same thought occurred to me when you recounted your tale of your companion's close relationship with the dolphins around your island. Ironically the name given to the order of sea mammals which includes whales and dolphins are Cetaceans."

I puckered my brow in puzzlement. I was being too bright. "Why ironic sir?"

"Well Cetaceans are named after the sea monster Cetus of course who, you may recall, was the monster to whom the princess Andromeda was chained to the sea cliffs in sacrifice. The reason for Andromeda's sacrifice of course was to appease the Nereids, for her mother, Queen Cassiopeia had boasted that she was more beautiful then they and they appealed to Poseidon to punish her for her vanity and arrogance by sending Cetus to ravish her country. Thus Andromeda was offered up in sacrifice." Dr Theodorakis chuckled softly. "It would appear that Nereids are bad people to cross!"

"I've heard of other mythical Greek sea creatures sir. Aren't there also sea nymphs known as Oceanids?"

Dr Theodorakis nodded gravely. "Indeed there are although the Oceanids are not so exclusively associated with the sea as the Nereids. The Oceanids were the three thousand daughters of the god of the great seas, Oceanus. and his sister Tethys. Poseidon was the god associated with the Mediterranean incidentally and Oceanus, from where we derive the term ocean naturally.

was more a god of the realm of the world ocean which, to the ancients was most closely represented by the body of water we now call the Atlantic Ocean. Poseidon of course became the god Neptune in the Roman pantheon and it is a tradition to this day to invite the god Neptune aboard ship when crossing the equator. That however is, strictly speaking, incorrect, since the equatorial regions of the oceans are not within the dominion of Poseidon or Neptune and one should correctly call upon the god Oceanus since that is his territory."

I cleared my throat loudly. Dr Theodorakis was wont to ramble off along many convoluted side paths unless occasionally brought back to the point. "But the Oceanids sir?" I reminded him.

"Ah yes. Well of course the Oceanids were another manifestation of sea nymphs of course and frequently in the company or close association with sea gods and the Nereids. They were not entirely confined to the seas however for they also inhabited rivers, lakes, pond and even marshes and clouds. Each one would be the patron of a particular body of water; a sea, a bay, a river, stream or lake or some such."

I bit my lip in uncertainty. "Could their individual association with a particular body of water be interpreted to have originated in sea nymphs' territorial behaviour?"

Dr Theodorakis stroked his chin thoughtfully. "Well it is purely speculation of course but the idea is a fascinating one. Your companion's territorial dominion over her island and surrounding sea certainly tallies with my own observations. It seems that small family groups have very marked territories and I rather think that unmated individuals, which I believe your companion to be, may well move away from their families to establish their own territories. If our observations are true then it would be logical that individuals would become associated with particular geographical locations and thus, in folklore, deemed to be the patrons of those

160

regions. Then there is the problem of the Naiads who are often considered to be the daughters of Oceanids and more closely associated with fresh water such as springs, streams, brooks and wells. In olden times every spring was considered to be protected by its local Naiad and if she were to abandon it, it was thought that it would dry up."

I thought of the curious pool of fresh water on the island whose source I had never determined and shivered involuntarily. I shook my head; myth and reality becoming confused within my thoughts. "So the various water nymphs are classified through their association with fresh or salt water then?"

Dr Theodorakis shook his head. "Not entirely. Certainly the Nereids, Sirens and Oceanids seem more connected to seas than Naiads but there is always considerable overlap. You must remember that, to the ancients, the water of the world consisted of a single system and that the fresh water on land was merely the sea percolating through the ground into the land. They would not have had such a clear distinction between the salt water of the sea and the fresh water of a river other than whether one was potable or not. My point is that, wherever water occurred, there are these fabled creatures associated with it. We may be seeing that the origin of all these myths is founded in the actual existence of a truly aquatic hominid species such as we have both observed."

"There are powerful anthropological links in ancient Greek mythology to human like sea deities and their offspring. Even the goddess Aphrodite, later to be the Roman goddess Venus, emerged from the sea for she was born when Cronos cut off Uranus' genitals and cast them into the sea. Legend has it that she emerged from the sea at a rock just off the shore at Pafos in Cyprus called Petra tou Romiou, or the rock of the Greeks and sometimes called Aphrodite's Rock. It is something of a tourist destination these days!"

I blinked at the new thought. "So the goddess of love was a sea creature."

"Originally I suppose so, yes. Interestingly one of her children by Hermes was the minor deity Hermaphroditus, a being who became both male and female after a union with the Naiad Salmacis, who tried to rape him. Curious don't you think?"

My head was starting to spin. How the ancient Greeks ever kept tabs on all the daily doings of all their deities and offspring was a mystery. I tried to clear my head. "So what you are saying is that all these myths and legends had a foundation in truth?"

"Many old legends have a basis in truth Miss Delmonte; even some of the most fantastic ones. Take the legend of the fall of Atlantis for example. For centuries Atlantis has been considered a myth recounted by Plato in the fourth century BC and in all probability of no factual truth. Plato himself asserted that he first heard the story via Egyptian records. Nowadays however many scholars believe that his story is a mythological retelling of an actual event; the destruction of the Minoan civilisation following the volcanic eruption of the island of Thera in the seventeenth century before Christ. I myself am in two minds about it but certainly the Thera eruption was probably the greatest in human history and the resulting destruction and tsunami coincided with the collapse of the Minoan culture and was almost certainly responsible for it. It is by no means infeasible that the tale persisted in memory and folk lore to metamorphosise into the Atlantis legend."

"Myth and history are so closely interwoven it is often very difficult to tell one from another. The ancients were not known for their devotion to verifiable historical fact Miss Delmonte. Their myths, poetical interpretations, the squabbling of their gods and their morality bedevil us to this day. How much of the story of the Trojan War is historical fact? We may never know

162

but many scholars believe that such an event really happened although the actual details of the story that have been handed down to us are almost certainly fictitious. These people saw their Gods as continual participants in everyday life and did not have our modern sensibility to distinguish fact from the supernatural. We live with the consequences of that still. Most of the religious faiths extant in the world are, after all, based in the body of myth, superstition, belief in the supernatural and folklore of our ancestors. Trying to pick out the reality from these myths is an endless and seemingly hopeless task."

I wiped a hand across my brow. "But nevertheless you are saying that the ancients knew of her people and wove stories about them into their mythology."

"Such would be my best guess Miss Delmonte. There are just too many parallels between them and the ancient stories. It is not only Greek mythology that is rich in stories about such creatures either. Many cultures with close association with bodies of water have equivalent myths and legends. In fact, the prevalence of legends regarding mermaids and such like creatures around the globe is quite striking and the similarities between the legends are rather singular. Mermaids were long coveted in China for instance as a source of pearls but they were considered dangerous for it was feared that their songs could send men into a coma and drown them. There are many stories regarding the hypnotic power of the mermaid's song."

I held up a hand. "Wait a minute. Aren't mermaids supposed to be half fish, half human."

"Well in many tales yes, but not necessarily so. Certainly there seems to be no question that most of the aquatic people of Greek legend are completely human like. As to other versions that describe them as half fish well that could simply be a garbled description to account for their prodigious proficiency in water. We

163

often describe somebody who is exceedingly comfortable in water as saying that they swim like a fish. It is only a short step from there to describe them as half fish. There may be another explanation as well. Allow me to show you something."

Dr Theodorakis rose from his chair and stepped over to a large cabinet. From its interior he extracted a remarkable object. As I examined it its purpose was evident. It was a large fin like paddle made of some stiff material and apparently designed to fit on a person's feet like the mono-fins worn by free divers. "I took that from one of the islands where I often observed these people Miss Delmonte and I occasionally observed them using such aids, especially on deep dives. It seems to be made of sealskin as far as I can tell. If the use of such artefacts were common among them it is easy to imagine how unlearned, superstitious observers of old would interpret such a sighting and believe them to be half fish. Interestingly most depictions of mermaids show them to have their tail fins held horizontally to their bodies and to propel them by means of vertical strokes in the same way as a dolphin. Fish of course carry their caudal fins vertical to their bodies and move through the water by means of lateral strokes. Only mammals show the vertical undulations of the spinal column as opposed to the lateral ones you would see in a fish or reptile."

"So the accounts of mermaids being half fish could simply be misinterpretation."

"Quite so although the Assyrian goddess Atargatis, one of our earliest accounts of a mermaid from around 1,000 BC was described as half fish."

"And these legends are worldwide then?"

"Absolutely. Nearly every society with close connections to the sea has such stories. As you can well imagine they are particularly prevalent among people who live among island archipelagos. In the Caribbean for instance the mermaid is known as Aycayia among the

Neo-Taino nations and, in more modern culture, as Lwa La Sirene and the goddess or orisha common to both Caribbean and African devotees of the Yuraba religion called Yemaya is depicted as an aquatic sea deity. Sirena are part of the folklore of the Philippines and a beach in southern Java is reputedly the home of the mermaid queen Nyi Roro Kidul, a powerful figure in Javanese mythology."

"It is not only the islands of tropical regions or warm seas, such as the Mediterranean, that harbour such tales either Miss Delmonte. There are fables from much colder climates. In the Norman chapel of Durham Castle in England is an artistic representation of a mermaid dating to 1078. Then the Irish have the mermaid Li Ban who predates Christianity in Ireland and was, in some versions, reputed to be the sister of the sea goddess Fand. Interestingly another version of the story has Li Ban associated with a large body of fresh water, Lough Neagh in Northern Ireland. Incidentally the name Li Ban may have its etymological roots in the proto-Celtic word leiabannia meaning woman of liquid. Then again Scots have their own mermaid called Ceasg or Maid of the Waves and there are parallels with mermaid traditions in the Japanese ningyo."

Dr Theodorakis paused for a moment to sip his brandy and collect his thoughts. "I could continue along these lines indefinitely Miss Delmonte. I have made a study for many years of these stories. They are not confined to oceanic environments by any means. Many large lakes and river systems have their own legacy of such tales. We need only think of the Lorelei and Rhine Maidens of the river Rhine which are water nymphs out of Nordic myth and I have recently come upon certain stories out of African and South American river systems. My point, however, is that all this mythology adds up to a universality of the basic theme common to nearly all human cultures. I conclude therefore that these stories are so prevalent because they do in fact refer to actual, factual evidence; the evidence of human contact with a closely related, but separate, aquatic hominid species with which we have co-inhabited this planet alongside for many thousands of years.

I stared at him in astonishment. "You think they are an entirely different species from us then?"

"Absolutely. I think the anatomical differences alone are sufficient evidence of that."

"But...but how can that be? I mean how can an entirely separate human species live alongside of us?"

"It is not without precedent Miss Delmonte. Modern humans or Homo sapiens coexisted with Homo neanderthalensis, Neanderthal man, for many thousands of years. We might possibly have been instrumental in the extinction of the Neanderthal man. We might even have interbred with them."

"But weren't they just primitive ape men?"

"Not at all. They were highly developed intelligent hominids; technologically and socially on a par with early Homo sapiens and with a larger brain capacity. They were a kindred species to our own. We could have communicated with them. We most probably did."

"But surely we know of them from the fossil record. Why don't we have records of this species we're talking about in the fossils?"

"Many people, with little knowledge of anthropology, Miss Delmonte grossly overestimate the extent of our fossil records. In fact there are enormous gaps in our understanding of other hominid species. Many species of hominids we only know from small, incomplete fragments of a single fossilised skeleton. You have to remember that it is very difficult to become a fossil. You have to die in exactly the right place under exactly the right conditions for your remains to become preserved as a fossil. Such conditions may occur less than one time in several millions and there may be whole families of animals that existed of which we have no knowledge whatsoever of because we have never found any fossilised remains of them."

"Hominid remains are particularly scarce because, until the population explosion of our own species, the actual populations of them were so small. At the greatest height of its distribution, it is likely that the population of Homo neanderthalensis never exceeded more than one hundred thousand individuals; about the same as a small city and this over a range including all of Europe, the Middle East and extending as far east as the Ural Mountains and Afghanistan. We didn't even find a fossil of them until 1829 in the Neander valley in Germany despite them having inhabited a region that is one of the most densely populated on the planet."

"Hominid remains are very rare Miss Delmonte. I have heard it said that you could fit all the fossil remains, from every museum in the world, of hominid species other than our own, into the back of a small lorry. A species such as we're talking about that lives in tiny populations in the sea.... well the chances of finding fossil remains must be very low indeed. We don't even know if they bury their dead. For all we know their dead are simply eaten by crabs."

"But I presume Neanderthal man died out many thousands of years ago..."

"About 25,000 thereabouts Miss Delmonte."

"But you're saying that here is another hominid species which has survived into modern times."

"Yes. It may seem fantastic but again there are precedents. There has been speculation for many years that other hominid species have survived until relatively modern days. There are innumerable stories of cryptid hominids from around the world; the Yeti of the Himalayas, the Almas of the Caucasus and Pamir mountains, the Barmanou of Afghanistan and Pakistan, the Batutut of Vietnam, Laos and Burma, even your own

167

North American Bigfoot Miss Delmonte; the list goes on. Now of course many of them may be simple legend or folk tale or even a hoax yet there are a surprising number of them from around the world. Nevertheless it would be tempting to dismiss them all as pure fantasy; pure fantasy if...." Dr Theodorakis slapped his fist into his palm for emphasis, "if you and I did not have the evidence of our own eyes to tell us that there is indeed another species of humankind alive in this world at this very time. Make no mistake about it Miss Delmonte. You and I are both privileged to have witnessed something extraordinary... the proof, the undeniable proof that the human race is not alone; that a kindred species lives, walks and swims in the waters of our world even as we speak."

I remember my mind reeling at the implications and yet everything the Doctor said made complete sense. Still I had difficulty grasping the concepts however. "But sir," I protested, "We are talking not about a Neanderthal man here but a completely aquatic human species. Is that at all likely?"

"I hardly see why it should be considered unlikely at all Miss Delmonte. After all we have the very close analogy of our own species."

"What do you mean?"

"I mean Miss Delmonte that our own species is itself partly aquatic. We think of ourselves as terrestrial animals but in fact we are almost unique among primates in our affinity to water. Find a body of water on the planet and you'll find human beings, bathing in it, swimming in it, fishing in it or simply basking by the side of it. We are aquatic creatures Miss Delmonte. Our natural habitat is along the side of water. It is estimated that some eighty percent of the human race lives within two hundred kilometres of the sea. We even seem designed for a semi aquatic lifestyle. Our very hairlessness could be an adaptation to an aquatic existence. No other primate, recognised by science, is at home in water. When did you last see a chimpanzee swimming? You can even drop a human baby into water and it will swim quite happily. Its aquatic nature is built into its genes. The female of our species, curiously enough, is particularly well adapted for swimming. Ladies are generally more buoyant and carry insulating layers of sub-cutaneous fat, allowing them to dive deeper into cold water than men, which is why women are used as pearl divers in many cultures.

What I mean to say Miss Delmonte is that not only is an aquatic hominid completely possible it may be that these people are, in fact, more closely related to us than other extinct and more terrestrial hominids that we know from the fossil record."

"Other hominids aren't hermaphroditic." I pointed out.

Dr Theodorakis nodded to acknowledge the justice of my observation. "You are right Miss Delmonte... or at least right as far as we know. I must confess that that is something that I have long thought about. Hermaphroditism is common in nature but generally not so among higher invertebrates. There are examples of course. Those sea bream that you caught on your island for example are known to be hermaphroditic. Many live lives as a female and then, for reasons unknown, suddenly change into males. Still I concede that it is pretty much unknown among mammal species. Nevertheless there is no natural law that renders it impossible. Indeed hermaphroditism on an individual basis is well known among mammals including humans even if it isn't a characteristic of the species. Surprising numbers of humans are born with ambiguous genitalia and among some specialist who have studied the question it appears that the distinction between male and female genders is not anything like as clear cut as once fondly believed.

I have a colleague, with whom I correspond regularly, who is of the opinion that we are on the brink of a revolutionary new field of human study that will call into question all our notions about human sexuality and gender. They believe that such things, currently regarded, by medical science and society as a whole as aberrant behaviour or conditions, such as homosexuality and trans-sexuality, will sometime in the near future be regarded as completely natural circumstances of the human condition. Doubtless there will be opposition to such radical notions from the ingrained moral bigotry of those who resist such challenges to their fervently held beliefs but societies can and must evolve. If it is true that sexuality and gender identity are more fluid in human beings than we currently believe then is it so radical to imagine a closely related species in which the distinctions are even less clear cut? Well we have seen the evidence for ourselves Miss Delmonte."

By the more enlightened standards of the scientifically literate of our current age, Dr Theodorakis' statement does not seem at all progressive but this was in 1972 and the notion that being gay or transgendered was a natural human condition was damn close to being subversive back then. Of course it still is to some people but then there are still some people who believe the world was made in 6.000 BC and that Noah managed to collect several million species of animals on a wooden boat he built in his back yard because God was so pissed that he decided to flood the entire planet!

I leaned back in my chair to cogitate over the Doctor's remarks while he replenished our brandy glasses. We seemed to have wandered onto strange paths. I had some more personal questions to ask. "Forgive me sir," I ventured, "But we seem to have become side-tracked. You were telling me earlier that you had not had contact with these... these mermaid people for some years. I presume that I'm right in assuming that that changed this summer."

"You are quite right of course Miss Delmonte. I am sorry if I have digressed into a more general analysis of your companion's people. It is true that I owe you something more by way of explanation." He leaned back thoughtfully to marshal his thoughts. "Let me see now. I think it was around the beginning of July that I first heard word that one of the sea people was once again close by. I heard a story that two local fishermen had heard an unworldly singing, near to some island over to the west. Well, of course, that intelligence galvanised me for it was years since I had last heard of any such report. I interviewed the two fishermen immediately. I'm afraid the experience had badly frightened them and I received only the most garbled and confusing information from them as to the exact whereabouts of the incident. Nevertheless I kept my ear to the ground as it were and I asked Dmitri to take his boat out to the west to see if he could learn anything.

Dmitri's initial reconnaissance proved to be futile however and, over the next weeks, I began to think it was a false alarm. Then one evening as I was sitting in my garden I heard a brief snatch of song myself. Even after all those years, I recognised it immediately. It was a short song, more of a cry, that the sea folk used to use to alert me to their presence when I was a youngster and traded with them. I knew I was being called. The sound seemed to come from the little headland just on the bay here and I set off immediately to investigate it. There, perched on a rock close by the water's edge, was the person you have spent the summer with.

I cannot begin to explain how ecstatic I was to see one of her kind again for I'd thought them lost to me for good. She was waiting for me but she seemed nervous and unsure. I think she must have learned the call that summonsed me from others of her kind that knew me and trusted me but she had little way of knowing my identity herself. I put her at her ease by vocalising some of the sounds I had learned from her people and she relaxed visibly. It seemed she wanted to trade for she held out some small but beautiful pearls.

It was difficult to know what she wanted in exchange however. Although I had learned tiny fragments of her tongue as a young man, and tried to expand it through my brief contacts over the years, I cannot with any justification say that I speak her language or even begin to understand its structure. Nevertheless, after much gesticulation and hard work it became apparent that she wanted food. This surprised me for I well knew that her kind were more than capable of feeding themselves from the bounty of the sea. I had assumed that she would want manufactured artefacts such as tools and so forth but no, it seemed she wanted food. It wasn't just any food she required either for she appeared to have specific requirements.

Finally, at an impasse, I led her back to the house. It was nearly dark by then and I dismissed the servants while she concealed herself in the bushes around the back. When all was clear she approached the house. She wouldn't come indoors for they are most wary in that regard but squatted outside while I brought her some samples of food to choose between. Her choices surprised me for some of them were not types of food I would normally associate with her kind such as fruits, vegetables and even a sack of flour."

I laughed at this point. "I wondered where she got that from sir. I have to thank you. I used it to bake bread with. You've no idea how good plain bread tastes when you haven't seen any for months on end."

"It is my pleasure entirely Miss Delmonte. Of course, since listening to your account, I understand that she was foraging for food for you and, even then, I rather suspected that she had ulterior motives for her shopping list as it were. I am still amazed that she knew what flour was for. I didn't send her away with just foodstuffs however for I was keen to re-establish contact. I let her have a few other trinkets as well including an old but good quality filleting knife and a little hand axe."

I nodded. "Yes I remember them sir. That little axe was most useful. We used it to chop up driftwood and cut firewood in the olive grove."

"I'm gratified to hear it Miss Delmonte. Well you can imagine my pleasure at once again having made contact with her kind. I tinkered with the idea of taking a boat out to see if I could locate where she was living but in the end I thought perhaps such an intrusion might scare her away and so I discreetly left her in peace although I did start to leave tokens for her by the rock on the headland where we first met. As you by now will surely have realised she visited me several more times, calling out for me from the headland usually after dark and I furnished her with more supplements to your diet as well as other things."

"By this time I was pretty sure that she was obtaining food for somebody else and I rather suspected that the other person was a human. Certainly there are old stories of sea nymphs capturing people and keeping them alive. There were stories told among the older people, when I was a child, of young people being kidnapped by the sea folk and held captive on remote islands for terrible purposes that were only whispered about."

I shrugged. "Hey it wasn't that bad. I kind of got to enjoy it once I got used to it."

Dr Theodorakis rubbed his chin austerely. "Yes, er quite. Anyway my suspicions were, to some extent, confirmed only rather recently when Dmitri came to me to report that he'd seen a young woman, without any clothes on, on a small remote island over to the west. He was able to view her with his binoculars but I'm afraid he was rather too frightened to investigate too closely or

173

he might have rescued you earlier."

I grimaced wryly. "It was probably for the best sir. She was pretty protective of me. I hate to think what she might have done if somebody had tried to steal me away. I guess she could be pretty dangerous if anybody invaded her territory like that. She might have even killed him. She was certainly strong enough and aggressive enough."

"Yes those were indeed my own thoughts Miss Delmonte. I am quite aware how dangerous they can be when they or their territory and property are threatened. On the other hand I knew from Dmitri's report that the young lady on the island did not match the description of the person who was trading with me."

"I'm surprised that I never saw Dmitri's boat."

"He was very discreet, he led me to believe, approaching without engines at dusk behind some outlying rocks. He was most nervous I understand."

"She would have known he was there."

"Yes I concur. It did leave me with a dilemma however. I considered it likely that the person Dmitri had seen was an ordinary human being, if you'll pardon my saying so, and most likely the person for whom she had obtained food. I think that, more or less, confirmed her base of operations as it were. It occurred to me that the person might be in need of er... some assistance but on the other hand I didn't want to charge in and possibly endanger lives. I instructed Dmitri therefore to keep some distance while I endeavoured to make inquiries about the possible identity of the person being held on the island. That proved to be difficult for I could find no report of anybody reported missing locally.

"Then, one day, I chanced to talk with the captain of one of the local ships servicing the island while they were anchored up here and he casually mentioned a colleague of his whose ship had apparently lost a young American tourist overboard, who had vanished without trace, in the spring. I made some discreet inquiries and it seemed that the young person in question was a young lady but it seemed improbable, at first, that the person could be the same one that Dmitri had reported seeing for her disappearance had occurred a great distance away. Nevertheless I could find no other report of any missing person that matched the description of the young lady Dmitri had reported seeing on the island so I resolved just a few days ago to attempt to positively identify her.

My resolution was forestalled however. Just within the last days your erstwhile companion arrived once more in the dead of night and summoned me to the shore with her cry. She did not want to trade this time however and indeed she seemed most agitated. It took a long time to gather exactly what she wanted and in the end she led me quietly to the harbour and pointed at Dmitri's boat which she by now obviously associated with me. She conveyed to me that she wanted the boat to follow her to her island and at last I discerned that it was possible that she wanted to surrender her er... companion if you like to us.

I gave Dmitri explicit instructions to follow her although he was most anxious about the business. She paddled ahead in her canoe so as to retain visual contact, Dmitri tells me, but when she put into the island he hesitated long before daring to approach. Possibly it was my fault for not accompanying him but I thought to maintain a discreet distance. At length it seems he summoned the courage to put into the island himself although he tells me he was most keen to get away from there quickly. The rest of course you know." Dr Theodorakis took a rueful breath. "I must apologise therefore Miss Delmonte that we were so tardy in coming to your assistance after I had discovered your existence. I can only say in my defence that things were not quite so clear and it was difficult to know how to

175

proceed."

I nodded numbly and stared for long seconds into the glowing embers of the fire. The flickering light of the flames on the walls of the room reminded me of the light of our little cooking fires in the ruins of the old villa on the island. Finally I shook my head with a gnawing feeling of loss within me. "You have nothing to apologise for sir." I said quietly at last. "I was in no need of rescue. Has she been able to take me with her when she left I would have chosen that rather than return to the life I left behind sir. You may think me crazy sir but, in a strange way, I loved her. I would have stayed with her forever."

Dr Theodorakis nodded solemnly. "I see." he said quietly. "I repeat Miss Delmonte....I envy you." For long seconds we remained silent gazing into the fire. Finally he cleared his throat. "But return you did Miss Delmonte and that leaves me with a problem."

I blinked in surprise. "A problem?"

"Yes Miss Delmonte. Naturally we must endeavour, tomorrow, to inform the authorities that you have been found and expedite your reunion with your family who must be sorely missing you. It is that which causes me concern. I am going to ask you to do something very hard Miss Delmonte; in fact I am going to beg you. It may seem an onerous thing to ask of you but I assure you that I have only the very best motives for doing so."

"What is it you require of me sir?"

"I am going to ask you to keep the story you have told me tonight secret. Doubtless when we contact the authorities they will wish you to make a statement to account for your whereabouts over the last months. I want you to give them an edited version of the truth; a version that makes no mention of your companion or her kind. It is important, no, it is imperative that you tell nobody what truly occurred during these past months. I do not ask this for my benefit you must understand but rather for the benefit of that person you have told me you love; for her and for all her kind."

I was puzzled. "But why sir?"

"How many of her kind do you think there still are Miss Delmonte?"

"I... I have no idea."

"Few Miss Delmonte... very few. I think once they were more numerous especially here in the Aegean and in the Mediterranean at large. I have a theory that these warm seas were once the centre of their distribution. Certainly the prevalence of stories about them in the Mediterranean suggest that this region was particularly important to them. Also the environment with many small islands in a warm, relatively shallow sea with little in the way of tidal currents and with a benign climate would have been eminently suitable habitat for them. Unfortunately the environment also favoured the growth of human civilisations around these waters and that probably contributed to their decline. In our modern world the pressures on their environment must be enormous."

"If, as I suspect, there were races of them that occupied fresh water habitats, then those have almost certainly dwindled to vanishing point with the pressure on river systems and inland lakes. Perhaps there are isolated colonies of them along remote rivers in the tropics such as the Amazon or the African rivers. I sincerely hope so. As to their marine environments then there is still perhaps some hope that a few small pockets of them exist. I think the colonies in the Caribbean are probably extinct or verging on extinction and those in the Mediterranean are very nearly so as well. I consider it likely that no more than a handful of them are still extant in the entire Mediterranean. My best hope for some surviving remnants of their kind are among the Pacific islands of Micronesia but even they must be declining alarmingly."

"I feel it, deep in my bones, that we are seeing the very last of a dying species. You and I Miss Delmonte might be among the last people ever to know this remarkable race of creatures. We may have looked for the last time upon a species doomed to extinction. What a terrible loss that would be to the world. How will we face our children's children knowing that we allowed the one other intelligent creature on this planet who we could truly meet as equals to vanish and leave us alone after all?"

Dr Theodorakis paused for several seconds but I could see the sadness in his face as he contemplated that terrible loss. At last he mustered the composure to continue. "I have made it my life's work to study these people Miss Delmonte for I have always known that it was possible that whatever I learned of them might be the final legacy I could leave to posterity to let the world know that such people once existed; the final chapter in their long story if you like. I have not been alone in this endeavour I must confess. There are a few of us around the world aided and assisted by a private and very secret foundation who have made it our business to study these people and, if at all possible, to preserve them and ensure that, in a world dominated by our own species, there is still a place left for those kindred people of ours. It would be an honour for me to invite you into our select ranks Miss Delmonte and I think, with the deep sympathy you have so clearly demonstrated for those people, you will find accord with our principles and motives."

"And you think sir that by publicising the existence of those people; bringing them to public knowledge, I might endanger their chances of survival?"

Dr Theodorakis looked at me keenly. "You are a remarkable young lady if I may say so Miss Delmonte. You see the problem clearly I think. If we were to give the authorities a full, unedited and truthful account of your adventures then, assuming it was believed, there would be a sensation. You can imagine that every last island in these waters would be scoured for them, there would be fear and xenophobia on the one hand, eager scientists and anthropologists keen to make their reputation on the other, thousands upon thousands of merely curious sightseers swarming about their habitat on the chance of seeing them. You might even imagine tour operators running trips, television crews, even people wishing to capture live or dead specimens. They are not a species that could handle such pressure Miss Delmonte. Therefore if you love her, if you truly love her, then keep her secret lest we unleash an avalanche that drives a fragile, endangered species over the brink of extinction and the song of the Siren will be lost to us forever."

I can still remember sitting horrified in Dr Theodorakis' study listening to those ominous and sonorous proclamations of doom and I understood. Just a few months ago I had had no idea that any such people as her even existed but now I saw what a great, lonely place this world of ours would be without her. There was never any question that I would accede to Dr Theodorakis' request. I would keep her a secret between us and hope that somewhere, on a rock beside some beautiful island, she and her kind would sing on into a brighter future for both our peoples.

Later we retired to bed but I had trouble getting to sleep with all the thoughts in my mind and the unfamiliar comfort of the big bed. I suppose I drifted finally into a fitful slumber punctuated by strange dreams. In those dreams I fancied I heard her song drifting across the waters to me. I awoke with a start but there was no sound other than the ticking of the big old fashioned clock in my bedroom. I rose from my bed and took a chair by the window overlooking the sea. It was cool in the room so I wrapped a blanket about myself.

The moon was nearly full and the sea shone in a pearly radiance under its illumination. I sat there for many hours gazing out to sea.

Chapter Fifteen

There's little more to tell in my Aegean story. The next day Dr Theodorakis was true to his word and we endeavoured to get in contact with the authorities. There were no cell phones in those days, of course, and the islands relied on a rickety network of submarine telephone cables and radio sets to communicate with the mainland. We did succeed at length in contacting higher authority and we sent telegrams to the American embassy in Athens and to my parents' home in Iowa. My parents thought I was dead, of course, and the memorial service for me had been conducted long ago. My mother nearly fainted when they received the telegram and my dad thought at first that it was some kind of sick joke. When they were finally convinced that I was indeed alive and well they determined to fly straight out to Greece to bring me home in person.

This all took some time however and I spent several days at Dr Theodorakis' home. We spent the time in devising and polishing a heavily edited account of my adventures but I also committed as much of my true story and observations to paper as I could in the time for the Doctor's records. Other than that we spent much time in deep conversation either in his study or in long walks about the island. I remember for instance one day having a long talk with him whilst walking along the cliffs overlooking the sea. Dr Theodorakis was unconvinced that the organs on her neck and shoulders were gills for that would be unprecedented among mammal species. I argued stringently that that is what they were. I had seen them in action. It was something we were never to quite agree upon.

I was also obliged to write a statement for the police. It was a fictitious document. We invented a tale of pure fantasy that I'd been stranded alone on the island with no means of escape and survived on my own native wits until fortuitously discovered by Dr Theodorakis' employee. I had to repeat this story both to the police authorities in the islands and again back on the mainland. I think the police thought it too fantastic to be true. If they'd known the real story they might have locked me up in an asylum.

When I finally took a ship back to the mainland, Dr Theodorakis insisted upon accompanying me. Mom and Pa had flown into Athens the day before and we met them at their hotel. Mom threw herself on me and wouldn't let go of me for the rest of the day. Pa was torn between crying and raging about the incompetence of the Greek authorities that had abandoned his beloved daughter, stranded on a barren island to fend for herself. The authorities themselves seemed deeply suspicious of my story but they were under pressure from the American embassy and my father, who was threatening to sue everybody he could think of, and so they were eager to see the back of me. I guess they were pretty embarrassed the obvious incompetent bungling of the investigation into my disappearance. Thus the bureaucratic haggling was kept to a minimum and within two days I was saying goodbye to Dr Theodorakis at Athens airport. I promised to stay in touch. It was a promise I was to keep for I corresponded with him regularly until the day he died and visited him on several occasions in the future.

The flight home was tedious but my arrival back in the states caused something of a stir. The whole town turned out to welcome me home with a big party and I had my name in the newspapers and even on television. They were calling me Delilah Crusoe; the all American girl that vanished in the Aegean Sea and survived all on her own on a desert island. I could have sold the film rights for a small fortune if I'd had the stomach for it. I never told anybody that their "Delilah Crusoe" was more of a girl Friday. By odd coincidence I actually retraced the dates that I disappeared and it turned out that I actually did arrive on my island on a Friday.

When all of the brouhaha had quietened down I took some time out to re-evaluate my life and the direction it was going in. I'd grown up a lot on that island. I decided to go back to college. I majored in mythology. Pa was horrified. I think he wanted me to go to law school. Law school! God I'd have died of boredom! My correspondence with Dr Theodorakis helped me through college and I came out with first class honours. I studied natural history and anthropology in my spare time. I took my masters shortly after and then, with the authoritative recommendation of Dr Theodorakis and a goodly slice of financial help as well, I travelled to England to study for my PhD at Cambridge. That's how I became Doctor Delmonte and a lecturer in Greek mythology at Cambridge. Dr Theodorakis was immensely proud of me. He came to my Cambridge graduation. We got drunk together in the Pickerel Inn on Magdalene Street.

I'm still a lecturer at Cambridge and most of my colleagues and nearly all of my students think I'm as mad as a hatter which means I fit in just perfectly in England. I carried on the legacy of Dr Theodorakis' inspiration however and I've dedicated much of my life to the private study of the sea nymphs in both legend and verifiable fact. Dr Theodorakis, in fact, used me extensively as his research assistant in this field and helped finance many of my trips abroad to conduct field research on his behalf and the private foundation he represented. I never lost my taste for foreign travel and my researches have carried me to some of the most off the map places in the world. I've learned a lot since those days in the Aegean and much of it startling; too much, in fact, to include in this short account. My colleagues at Cambridge just thought I was conducting anthropological research into my specialist subject of the origins of mermaids and other like fabled creatures in primitive societies' mythology. Well I was, partly, but they'd have found conclusive evidence of my reputed eccentricity had they known why.

I had some real adventures on those field trips. I got chased by bandits in the Amazon, got treed by a bear in Alaska, fell afoul of the authorities in the Philippines, made love to a geisha in Japan, survived a major hurricane on an atoll in the Pacific, froze my butt off by the shore of Lake Baikal in Siberia, had a close encounter with an aggressive shark off the Great Barrier reef in Australia, nearly trod on a stingray in the Parana River in Argentina, damn near got caught up in a war in the South Atlantic and caught a nasty tropical illness in the Congo. Ah well.... it's been a good life.

The most amazing thing that happened to me on my travels abroad however was on one trip to the Far East when I got beached for a while in Bangkok. I was kicking my heels in town waiting for confirmation of my next destination from the foundation and I drifted down into the Nana Plaza district out of curiosity. I was sat in a bar watching a cabaret when I was approached by the most beautiful woman I had ever seen. Her name was Ngam, which was appropriate for it means beautiful in Thai. I bought her drinks and within an hour I was smitten. She worked as a cabaret artist and she'd won several beauty contests. I couldn't take my eyes off her.

If you're familiar with the seedier parts of Bangkok you'll pretty much have figured out where this is going. Ngam wasn't the name on her birth certificate. She'd been called Nai-thim by her parents and, if you know Thai, well that's a boy's name. She was what is called in Thailand a kathoey; a male to female transgender person. Thailand has probably the highest percentage of transgendered people by population of any country in the world and they are pretty much a feature of Thai society.

For all that however they still live on the fringes of society and most of them work in cabaret or the sex industry.

Ngam was the gentlest and kindest person I had ever met. I stayed in Bangkok for nearly six weeks and long before that I was hopelessly in love. That wasn't the remarkable thing however. The most amazing thing was that she fell in love with me as well. I took her home with me and a few months later I married her. Kind of ironic isn't it? I suppose we had a lesbian wedding but because she was still officially male on her birth certificate it was a completely legal wedding long before gay marriage was acceptable in a civil ceremony. My friends and colleagues at Cambridge and my family all thought I was round the twist. I couldn't have given a rat's ass what they thought. I was in love and, if it seemed a little unusual, well all I can say is that when your first marriage has been to sex crazed mermaid then anything else seems tame in comparison.

It was the best thing I ever did. Ngam has been the joy of my life to this day. We have two kids; a little orphan Thai boy we adopted and a girl I had myself through a sperm donor. Don't ask me who the donor was because I'll lie. Being married to a transgendered person got me more interested in the subject than ever. It may turn out to be completely irrelevant but I discovered that a notable feature among very young male to female transgendered children is an affinity for mermaids. Ngam's favourite fairy story as a child was "The Little Mermaid" by Hans Christian Andersen. For our honeymoon I took her to Copenhagen and we took photos of ourselves by the statue of the mermaid perched on her rock in Copenhagen harbour.

I've made many more trips to the Aegean since that summer of '72; mostly to visit Dr Theodorakis. Dr Theodorakis had maintained a watch on my island in my absence. Although he never met her again he left objects of value to her in her favourite hiding places that I told him about. It seems as if she must have visited the island seasonally for some years because the objects were removed. Occasionally she left small gifts in return. One of these touched me greatly for it was a small but intimate carving of two women in embrace fashioned out of ivory. There was a set of small markings on it which corresponded almost exactly to the markings on the amber figurine she carved for me at our strange wedding and gave to me when we parted. I knew then that that carving was meant for me and Dr Theodorakis agreed and sent it to me to join my few precious memorabilia of her.

After a few years however it seemed as if she stopped coming to the island. We have no idea why. Perhaps she died. In any case there is no evidence that the island has ever been visited by one of her kind since. The words of Dr Theodorakis came back to haunt me. Perhaps with her they were gone for good. The world seemed a poorer place.

I even took a boat out with Dr Theodorakis many years later to the island but it looked finally completely abandoned. There were no fresh carvings in the quarry, no new artefacts anywhere and the whole place had a feeling of desolation. To cap it all the little pool of fresh water had finally dried up. It was truly barren now. I was gripped in an awful melancholy and could not bear to stay.

Dr Theodorakis passed away after a short illness some five years ago. He was a ripe old age by then but still as lucid and as brilliant to the end. It felt with his passing as if a library of irreplaceable books had burned to the ground. He had no family and I was deeply touched when he left his house and the bulk of his estate to me in his will. Ngam and I use the old house as our summer retreat now and plan to retire there.

Most importantly of all, he left me much of his

accumulated research and papers on the sea nymphs; a gold mine of information and the steady fruits of a lifetime's dedication. There was something else he left me as well and, in truth, this was the most wondrous gift of all. He had never formally introduced me to the head of the foundation nor divulged the whereabouts of its headquarters although I had met some of his colleagues who conducted the research. Now on his death I was presented with a formal letter of introduction to the astonishing person who guided the foundation from her stately home in Northern England.

The obligations of secrecy prevent me from disclosing the name of this person but I can tell you in all honesty that she is the most incredible human being I have ever met. From her and from the archives of the foundation of which she is the patron I learned astonishing secrets; secrets that gave me hope again; hope that the people of my lady of the island might yet survive and that there were powerful forces working actively to protect them and prevent their diminishing into the obscurity of myth. I learned that there were more of them than Dr Theodorakis had ever dared hope and I learned too the secrets of their whereabouts.

That is why just a few months ago I found myself on a distant island where, after all these years, I heard the Siren's song once more. But that, as the saying goes is another tale and I'll tell you that another time.

Epilogue

The oceanic research vessel "Lady Shiro" lay at anchor a little off shore of the atoll; a gleaming white apparition on the boundless expanse of azure water. The Pacific Ocean, for once, was living up to its name for only the gentlest of swells stirred the surface to lap against the ships flanks. The flag of the parent company, "Amethyst International" hung limply at the stern in the sweltering tropical heat and the sliver of land to the west shimmered in the haze.

Amanda Elvert wiped a streak of perspiration from her brow and shaded her eyes from the sun to gaze into the east where a dark spot had appeared above the horizon and grew in size and took shape with each passing second. The temperature was searing on the after-deck and Amanda would far rather have spent the heat of the day in a comfortable air-conditioned cabin. There was no real reason other than courtesy demanding her presence out on deck but that courtesy was paramount. The humming shape approaching was carrying a legend. It would be unthinkable not to greet that legend.

She was not the only one to think that true for, waiting beside her was the ship's first officer and the head of the vessel's contingency of scientific research. Behind them stood a sizeable representation of the rest of the crew and research facility. It was a fitting welcoming committee.

Amanda turned to the first officer. "Are the stories about her true?" she asked.

The man shrugged. "Nobody knows but if only half of them are true....." he tailed off unable to think of a fitting comparison. He grinned suddenly. "I've met her before. She's a hell of a lady!"

The helicopter was on its final approach now, the

throb of its engines drowning the sounds of the waves slapping at the ship sides and the cries of the sea birds. It came in low over the stern, the down draft whipping the water below into a miniature storm flecked with white crests and frightening a pair of boobies which took to wing with indignant squawks. Amanda's hair lashed about her face and she clutched at her skirt against the hurricane blast from the rotors as the pilot eased his aircraft down onto the helipad.

Amanda watched as the small woman stepped from the helicopter and ducked under the spinning rotor. She was advanced in age but sprightly enough it appeared for there was a spring to her step as she crossed the helipad towards the welcoming group. Amanda strode forward to meet her thrusting out a hand in greeting. "Dr Delmonte," she called above the helicopter's noise, "Welcome to Clipperton Island!"

THE END